CROCOSMIA

PRAISE FOR *CROCOSMIA*

Read *Crocosmia* slowly: it will rearrange your heart and change your life.

—CASSIE THORNTON

A novel of revolutionary transition that achieves the impossible: not only charting the transformation of the mechanics of society, but the liberation of consciousness itself. Sentence by sentence, and in the impossible and enthralling architectures of each page, Miranda Mellis's *Crocosmia* is a treasure.

—JORDY ROSENBERG

What if art could save the world? What if all we had to do was let it? Two women, mother and daughter, move to the woods to escape dark forces that plague the mother's dreams. What follows is an incisive and beautiful meditation on imagination and intention in the Anthropocene. An apocalypse narrative infused with hope and a domestic story that shines a light on our collective power, *Crocosmia* functions in conversation with Jenny Offill's *Weather* and Debbie Urbanski's *After World* while existing in a universe all its own. This novel is a revelation.

—SARAH LABRIE

I read *Crocosmia* hungrily, in a stretch of "stolen" hours, feeling both held and fueled by its articulations of complex political desire confronting the lack—so named by Lauren Berlant—of "genres for transition." This utter gift of a book is soaked in intelligence, beauty, resistance, and loss; its blood is what spills when theory meets practice, its references help it breathe. Meanwhile, its sentences—like its characters—grow the genre they need.

—ANNA MOSCHOVAKIS

Miranda Mellis has written a philosophical novel with a metaphysical sense of humor. In it, we meet Jane, who thinks about everything, and her daughter Maya, who takes her place and continues to think. *Crocosmia* describes a certain way of love between a mother and daughter in which, above all, it is the capacity for thought that is handed down.

—SHAHRNUSH PARSIPUR

Wildly hopeful and ecstatic with language, *Crocosmia* offers a yearning, visionary dose of eschatological surrealism. With both care and verve, Miranda Mellis mixes poetry, philosophy, memory, and imagination to tell a story of intergenerational debts and obligations in the face of radical social transformation. *Crocosmia* glows in the night.

—ROY SCRANTON

Is there a way out? Mellis posits a miracle, a dream within, almost invisibled but not yet, of ecological and ethical wisdom and liberation. *Crocosmia* reminds us of the values we thought we had and, as its syncretic miracle blooms to show the way, could have again.

MIRANDA MELLIS

CROCOSMIA

A NOVEL

NIGHTBOAT BOOKS

NEW YORK

Printed in the United States

ISBN: 978-1-64362-275-0

Cover Art: *40 Love* by Xylor Jane, 2019, Oil on panel, 19 ¾ × 19 ¾ inches.
Courtesy of the artist and CANADA. Photography by Joe DeNardo.

Design and composition by Kit Schluter
Typeset in Hoefler Text and MENDL SANS

Cataloging-in-publication data is available
from the Library of Congress

Nightboat Books
New York
www.nightboat.org

The one who emerges . . . does not only call forth unto a system of just laws, but also to a land, a climate, a way of building, a way of rejoicing and feasting, a way of remembering the dead, and of dying.

—ALPHONSO LINGIS, *The Imperative*

I felt myself, in the darkness of my room, become a tree and even a tree struck by lightning: my arms lifted little by little and their movement became knotted like that of strong branches . . .

—GEORGES BATAILLE, *Inner Experience*

History is made of dreams that either come true or are thrown into the garbage.

—ETEL ADNAN, *Premonition*

Each epoch dreams the one to follow.

—JULES MICHELET, "Avenir! Avenir!"

A problem is always temporal. No problem is not a problem of time and therefore of purpose. If one's purpose is one's problem, one's problem is certainly one's purpose, like it or not. Our problems give us purpose, the question is whether we can fulfill this purpose by solving our problems.

Without these problems, what would our purpose be?

Do we fail to solve these problems because without them, we would have no purpose?

Or because problem solving is itself the problem?

Or do we fail to solve these problems because we don't agree on what they are? Or because we can't face the fact that even if we accept that they are our purpose, and do our best to solve them, we may not solve them, we may never solve them, which will have meant that our life was lived in the pursuit of the irresolvable?

Then our life will have been an unsolved problem, a thing thrown, a ball that is never caught, a house that is always falling, a life that is always disappearing.

I.

Maya sat by herself at a cooperative café, situated on an airy observation deck that encircled the enormous central stem of a giant 700-meter high crocosmia flower, its red, rain-glistened petals arcing overhead. The conical architecture reminded her of the old world's air traffic control towers. The rain had just stopped, and angled sun rays lit gossamer, dispersing clouds. Densely layered gardens spread out below. Monkeys, goats, foxes, bison, and elk played and meandered among palisades, between earthworks and ceremonial complexes. Nests, roosts, perches, and rookeries dotted the flowering tower where myriad birds of many sizes and colors gossiped eagerly, interrupting each other, or staring pensively. The passage she was just now reading from Vladimir Mayakovsky's *How Are Verses Made?* was apt for the view:

> *A change of plane from that in which an action or fact is situated, a certain distance, is indispensable . . . you have to stand back, at a distance equal to three times the size of the object. If you don't do that, you simply won't see the thing you're depicting. The bigger the thing or the event, the further you have to get away from it.*

Mayakovsky was speaking about the distance needed to perceive and depict one's time and place clearly. He enjoined the poet to take distance from their poems, which also applied to the art of revolution. Distance made the difference, even just a hair's breadth, a moth wing. A changing plane tilts the scales.

Distance, Maya thought, seems like a solution but then becomes a problem. Too far away, and you want to get close again, now the distance might be untraversable. You might not find a way back, like one of these dreams of trying and failing to get somewhere, one obstacle after another in the way, space itself deflecting you, something you can't stop falling out of. She'd had many dreams of endlessly departing, never arriving. It was always her mother Jane she was trying to get back to.

Maya caught a glimpse of herself in her simple dark blue jumpsuit. There she was, her long white hair in a ponytail, her backpack sitting on the ground next to her chair, reflected in the double-paned passive solar windows and open to the cooler air of the lower troposphere. She didn't recognize herself in the reflection. The face in the glass portrayed solidity, whereas the inside feel was fluid. She squeezed lemon into her glass and smiled at the water glinting in the light. Water. Lines from an old poem came to mind . . .

Of all the words
they've used for water
starlight was the first

Water, soft as breath. Water above, clear and delicious, water below, millions of years old, thousands of feet underground, had the texture of maple sap and turned orange when exposed to oxygen. No one would have predicted, in her childhood, that, as before the industrialization of the elements, they would be able to rely, once again, on water's abundance. By the time she was born human beings had taken so much groundwater that the very axis of the earth had been altered. Now good water flowed once more through the winding arteries of the living earth.

The crocosmia above was another miracle. Under open sky the sheer redness of their enormous petals gave shade to hillside dwellings below and cured ailments. Although knowing their provenance as no one else could (for her they were not enigmas), Maya reveled in their spectacular largeness and welcomed their largesse. Each of the seven regions where these and other enormous flowers appeared had an interpretive center underneath so people could both visit and study them, their petals flying like so many red banners. This was her first time seeing them, though they had appeared long ago when her mother, Jane, disappeared.

As she had countless times before—the waking mind repeats itself; the sleeping one tries new things; while colonial grids were dismantled, called down to earth, to reparation, and whale pods took back their oceans—she wondered where Jane was. She looked out over the plains below and read from her guidebook:

In the cosmogony of this emergent world, a recovering world, a remediating world, the crocosmia with its red plumage is among the guardians. The crocosmia, a revolutionary who stands for the many-as-one, arranges itself in a convivial cluster on a floral axis. The pattern of their arising represents renewal, earth-faith, and the redemption of red.

Maya had taken a funicular to the observation deck where one could admire the grandeur of the flaming crests from a floating, open-air café, designed by means of biomimicry to grow skyward along with the inflorescence.

Like all the architecture of the period, the built environment was temperate: cool when it was hot, warm when it was cold, notwithstanding the ongoingly kaleidoscopic climate: instead of summer, fall, winter, and spring, drought, fire, hurricane, and flood. Instead of seasons, collage. Instead of rhythmic cycles, erratic fragments.

The changing climate made of life one sudden moment after another. Contexts collapsed. Everything was *suddenly* . . .

She observed the co-workers who stewarded the place, cleaning, cooking, serving, resting, talking. *The construction and maintenance of the structure*, the guidebook said, *was a technical matter as well as an ethical one. Technique and ethics are inseparable.*

She read on and to her surprise, saw a name she recognized, someone her mother had studied with.

In the twenty-first century physicist and feminist philosopher Dr. Karen Barad taught that "matter is striated with ethics." This insight gave the basis for a climate model which would no longer be solely predictive but constructive. A climate model that coalesced into a single shimmering crystal of infinitely changing emergences and dynamics, best symbolized by the Vedic concept of Indra's net. The most accurate map of the world, as Jorge Luis Borges had written, was the world itself.

The guidebook went on to describe how the *building* (both a noun and a verb) was alive, adaptive, absorbed heat, metabolized waste, generated water and food.

To address the pathologies of infrastructure, the time had come for builders to become clairvoyants, for architects, seers, and farmers to collaborate, pin their sails together, relearn how to live reciprocally within medicinal dwellings capable of change, and of learning. The blueprint for building as healthcare consisted of a question: What agencies and services are missing?

Maya's own dwelling place, a bungalow in the forest, had originally been built modularly, quickly, and on the cheap without eternity in mind, let alone climate change. For as long as she had lived there it had been been coming loose at the seams, being unmade by thick rains, heavy and streaming. It was being overwritten by the weather, seeded generations ago.

Like me, she thought, like any body, inexorably it falls, a slow self-demolition.

The first time she realized the bungalow was shifting, she had been sleeping. She woke up to an unusual ringing patter. In the morning, she saw it: a cleft had opened under a corner of the foundation. The rain struck a length of newly exposed pipe, the source of the unfamiliar sound.

She walked around the house and wondered how to prevent it from sliding right off its foundation into the nearby ravine, which was to be avoided for obvious reasons, as well as one reason which wasn't obvious.

Maya knew the obvious is rarely truly obvious. Even the uncanny equations she had once studied with her mother, that showed our universe has the properties of a hologram, were spoken of in the non-mood of obviousness. The closer you look, the stranger the obvious is. For instance, the seawater and stardust in our bodies, Maya mused, our scapula like the wings of seabirds, our backs fluid and bony like a rocky creek along which time has braided a spine.

Yes, that things are not obvious is obvious, Maya knew, even the obvious reason that she should prevent the house from sliding into the ravine wasn't obvious to her. Why shouldn't it go the way of all things? Except there was a small cemetery down there, although no one had been buried in it for generations, nor had Maya ever seen, over decades of walking there, anyone else. Like a nurse on a hospital floor in the middle of the night, she, a stranger, tended the ancestral graves, decayed over time until they were almost indistinguishable from the microbial earth, the unsanctimonious land.

She alone sat at those few graves garlanded with rusty metal pendants. Desiccated bouquets dissolved on touch, left many decades ago by people whose descendants didn't know about them, not even of their nonexistence.

Grey headstones, smaller ones for infants, with tattering pinwheels, the rusty brittle scrape of an ancient wind chime, photographs once sealed into the headstones now effaced, ambiguous, anamorphic, and fungal. Death is an abstract expressionist, Maya thought, who paints forgetfulness. To be forgotten, to be unknown is to be abstract, a whorl of grain. Maybe all abstraction is this, the imageless image of what goes unremembered, unknown. A form changed beyond recognition.

Why shouldn't the faltering bungalow go, then? she asked herself. Along with Jane, along with her, and everything from the past? Why interfere?

In the long view, in the big picture, the fact that the house was sliding was insignificant. But in the near term, for her, was it not a problem? A problem from the future and the past, from above and below, from all directions, on its way, already here, and almost gone. The problem dissolved if one didn't bother to solve it. It became the given; ordinary. She thought of Kafka's parable: *Leopards break into the temple and drink all the sacrificial vessels dry; it keeps happening; in the end, it can be calculated in advance and is incorporated into the ritual.*

Perhaps the wet hand digging away under the house has designs more important than mine, Maya thought, as I have never known where things should be anyway.

She had lived there since she was fourteen, when she and her mother Jane first moved to the northern forest where the decrepit bungalow was sited, built from a kit in the 1950s, "Design no. 4132." An architectural form "in the Bengali style," the bungalow originated in eastern India, where monsoons came earlier every year and lasted longer, where cyclones grew larger and more destructive, storms undreamed of by its inventors.

The house had been listed as a "tear down." Jane bought it sight unseen for several thousand dollars. When Maya first saw pictures of it, she didn't hide her doubt. "There's a well there," Jane reassured her, "and a septic system. That's all we need. We can repair the rest. And it's in a forest." Maya didn't reply at first. Then she said, "I thought private property was theft?" "Yes," Jane replied, "and it is a disgustingly shallow relationship to the land which could never truly be private if it is alive. We just need to remember that in truth, we own nothing—the earth is not for owning."

Maya was troubled and unconvinced. "We can be hermits!" Jane tried to jolly her. "You love hermits."

It was true that Maya had been reading about solitaries, cave dwelling monastics, and the "desert mothers" of old, Syncletica, Sarah, and Theodora, mystics, hermits, and ascetics who sought the deserts of Egypt, Palestine, and Syria in the fourth century, forming communities or living as solitaries. These deserts that had once been a refuge for mystics were unliveable now, and new ones encroached in the equatorial regions. In those ancient years what was later called negative self-talk was known to be the voices of demons. Feelings from nowhere winged around the arc of the body and were treated as messengers. Shadowed caves were chapels, birds were couriers.

How isolated they had been in the forest when they first moved, Maya reflected, especially compared to the seven years prior when they had lived collectively, in a close-knit community, at a place called the Anarchstery, the happiest time of her life. She still remembered how shocked she was that they were leaving, how reluctant she had been to go. She had no say in it.

The move to the bungalow in the woods was a return to her infancy and early childhood, when they had also been alone, when single parenting and the isolation of families was status quo. But there was that intermediary period from age seven to fourteen when they had lived with others, and those were happy times. Everything hummed at the Anarchstery. Back then, she had looked forward to her life. She didn't worry about her body or her mind, she just threw herself into her days.

After the move to the bungalow in the woods, when it was just the two of them again, she and her mother Jane, Maya would wake to an obscure tension she couldn't understand or get rid of.

§

Maya resumed reading the guidebook, which speculated about where the crocosmia came from, with its gargantuan, blade-shaped leaves, bent into passages and walkways, twirled into ramps between ambiently, green-lit sleeping quarters.

The ideas that had arisen to try to explain the conjuncture of the mysterious bloom of seven immortal, enormous flowers that vaulted to the sky, known as the "second seven wonders," with the seven decapitations of seven heads of state, included the theory that the colossal flowers were memorials for those seven heads, whose names were never since written or spoken without a red line through them.

In a new iteration of the archaic practice of crossing oneself, or averting the evil eye, making geometric gestures to evoke protection, one wrote the names of the heads (and others of their ilk) with a line through it. To speak a name with a line through it, you kept your lips tightly closed, like a ventriloquist.

You knew when you overheard someone say a word in that mumbled, nasal, and garbled way that a world-killer was being mentioned. Contrarily, if one was speaking of a world-healer, one rounded one's cheeks and pushed one lips together, pursed as if for a kiss, so those names came out whistling and flutey.

Maya knew the second seven wonders were not memorials at all, rather they were alchemical. She recalled the memorial she and Jane had encountered driving through desertified borderlands on their way north, to move to the bungalow in the forest, when she was fourteen.

They had pulled over for a rest and to eat pomegranates. They walked along a dry creek bed looking for a shady place to sit and eat the sweet red seeds. There were a few parched trees. They were sitting on a flat rock under a fading, peeling madrone when Maya noticed a peculiar shape in an opening in a dusty field across from the creek. Once they had rested and eaten, they went to look and found an enormous circle made of piles of worn out, torn, and broken shoes. A sign nearby said that this monument was inspired by Mohsen Lihidheb, a Tunisian artist and postal worker whose years gathering and sorting letters went alongside his lifelong practice of picking up shipping matter that had washed up on the beaches of his coastal city of Zarzis and making art of what he found. His medium was loss.

Brined and hardened, the things Lihidheb gathered were sculptured by the sea and the sun. Piled up on the horizon, these were the belongings of people who had tried to migrate from regions where agriculture was first created, now deserts where farming was no longer practicable.

These descendants had left their ancestral lands in search of water, food, and safety. They lost their homes, and many lost their lives along the way. Lihidheb had created a museum he called "The Memory of the Sea" composed of all that he gleaned from the shore: clothes, shoes and, finally, as the militarization of borders had intensified, bodies, lost to their loved ones, and futures, and pasts, who he duly took it upon himself to honor with burial.

Maya and Jane kneeled and squatted down to look at the circle of shoes. A pair of tiny pink ballet flats, many crumpled sneakers, boots, sandals, clogs, flip flops, all gathered and carefully arranged by someone unnamed, who had been inspired by Lihidheb's "The Memory of the Sea." This shoe memorial was called, after Lihidheb, "The Memory of the Desert."

After a long time of looking at the memorial, Maya remembered how her mother had said, her loose black tunic billowing in the breeze, *He didn't wait for someone else to do it.*

§

Had Jane been the one wearing a black blouse that day, or had Maya been the one wearing it? The memory seemed as plain as day, as the saying went, replete with depth perception. The actual world, a cognitive process. She used to have an extraordinary memory. She could remember anything she wanted, even a dream she'd had thirty years ago. Now her memory had grown chaotic, and it was hard indeed to separate dreams from memories. Sometimes entire scenes of her life replayed in her mind with every detail intact. Other times, unrelated events would bump into each other and then seem coupled. As these different memories laminated, the past was fictionalized.

Nowadays as often as not memories simply eluded her. They rose up and then immediately slunk away, as if they couldn't be bothered, collapsing back into that vortex from which they inexplicably surfaced.

The café was full of old musicians who no longer had the strength for earth work. They had plenty of other ways to live and contribute. They worked on strategies and plans, played music, practiced the domestic arts, cooked, taught, danced, wrote, argued, traveled, and studied. Mostly, though, they played music. Everywhere you went elders could be found playing music of every kind, recovering time's plenty, tempo overflowing its banks.

Maya listened to one old timer playing piano while another drummed elliptically. As it always had, sound evoked color. She heard silkily threaded, intricate coalescences of bright green notes, call and response between silver and black, flashing silver dotted staccatos followed by winding blue spirals, then a sudden plunge down and level out into scattered flickering stars, finally a rising unity, a coordinated, single red flame of sound. She heard loud laughter from the kitchen, saw a burst of yellow confetti.

The climate was like this unpredictable music, despite the achievement of zero emissions, an achievement of absence. Here, *nothing* was the great accomplishment. Negation was never less philosophical, never less abstract. What had to be negated was omnicide.

The co-operative societies that had emerged in the last seventy years no longer burned fossil fuels, but still suffered "the sins of the fathers." The phrase lands with a thud, Maya thought, meaningless with overuse. Deuteronomy 24:16 stated that "Fathers shall not be put to death because of their children, nor shall children be put to death because of their fathers." But the children *were* put to death by physics that the fathers' denial—an upraised weapon, an egregore—manifested in the form of floods, hurricanes, fires, and heatwaves, demonstrating how mere ideas are sentient, cause events—are deeds.

Maya remembered studying extinctions with her mother. The ratios of survival were determined by quantifying the number and rate of migration corridors under composition, dismantled dams, open border walls, and closed highways, compared with the pace of heating, drought, and relative adaptability of species. Doing extinction math was like being in an ever-diminishing room in which everyone was talking at once. The voices got louder as the room got smaller. Before the Great Turning, world-girdling civilization had nearly lost the earthly plenitude known to prior generations. The bustling paradisical world-garden had become increasingly deserted but for the most versatile migrants and extremophiles.

But first in small groups, later in masses, soon most of human existence revolved around facilitating climate migrations, transitions off those civilizational constructs that produced carbon dioxide, methane, and nitrous oxide emissions, remediation and reforestation, water and land-healing. Communities organized to halt productivism and consumerism, to stop accepting the unacceptable, to shed that fearful, hoarding instinct that sunk all things to the lowest common denominator, "bottom line," to de-create capitalist empire and its car-serving ontology of pavements, "impervious surfaces" which caused flooding and killed soil, pavement that promised to keep people going to work forever, a commutation of the commute—the very death drive itself. What was once considered unexceptional shown in all its aberrance: that soil should be entombed; that rivers should be straightened to make fish swim faster to their slaughter.

Gradually, a less damaged and paranoid world. Quick and determined, slow and methodical. Detoxified land, de-acidified oceans, reparative mentalities. They rewove the soil, washed clear the atmosphere, harbored seeds instead of resentments, stopped counting down, unplugged the doomful temptation, turned it around, danced widdershins to counteract the Taylorist clock. Ecosystems were set free from industrial grids. Overworked, time itself breathed a sigh of relief as basic needs were met. Needs which were, in truth, not basic at all. They were the *baseline* of existence.

Though greenhouse gasses were no longer emitted anywhere,

the climate was still tumultuous with prior generations of emissions yet to be "drawn down" (as the saying went—as if ending a war).

The transition was underway, species returned, spores and pollen hopped and flew, oceans de-acidified, biodiversity was on the rise, air, water, and soil restored themselves, and the colors of biointelligence proliferated, aimless leisured green, black night and wings, flowered crowns of violet and golden beaded meadows, bright snaps of clear blue, humankind's innate love of every hue. An atmosphere clear of poisons and atavistic tensions as if the ancestors had discovered temperance—yet temperature still fluctuated outlandishly.

Planet-heating gasses, a literalization of the inflammation of a world in thrall to patriarchal hysteria, would be a long goodbye.

It was hard to believe how long they had held on, even as people went without shelter and starved. In 2023 a treacherous head of state had paid for a single missile what it would have cost to feed everyone in "his" country for a year. Maya's mother Jane had drawn Maya's attention to these sorts of facts at every opportunity when she was growing up: how states were always founded on violence, how they were predicated upon violence, war, arms trafficking, surplus populations, hunger, fear, and abandonment.

As a child, Maya was aware that Jane despised political parties, that she believed in their abolition because in the party system politicians were elected not based upon their actions, but merely because of their affiliations.

A system will always fulfill its purpose, Jane would say. *If you want to change a system, change its purpose. If a system's purpose is to elect a leader, the system will elect a leader. If a system's purpose is for political parties to compete, that is what the system will do. If a system is designed for the production and consumption of commodities, then it will do that. Even birth and death will be commodities. And all other purposes will be at the very least tertiary, if not destroyed.*

Maya had asked what the word *tertiary* meant. Jane pointed to the enormous, musty old dictionary that stood in the corner on its own dedicated stand next to shelves and shelves of hundreds of books they had rescued from dumpsters over the years. Relentless solar flares had caused libraries to regret deaccessioning books, and many of those who had held onto their collections opened them up to the public, so that they doubled on a scheduled rotation as libraries. Jane and Maya's apartment in Maya's early childhood was one such site.

Maya recalled how, when she leafed through that fossil of a dictionary and gently peeled its onion skin pages, she would sometimes lose track of her question, drawn in by thousands of other words, how they nestled near each other, their roots pointing to other languages, other dictionaries, each word made of other words, each dictionary connected to other dictionaries, meanings growing and changing over time, like ecosystems which had been studied in too much isolation. Understood in part and misunderstood in whole.

In that dictionary Maya had found unexpected beauty in the word *disaster*: dis / astro—*undone star* and more meanings than she had thought possible in the word *tree*, its meanings tree-like, branched. Tree was rooted in *trust*. Then there was the variety of flora: trees in the plural. There was the *circulatory* tree: the tree of life. There was the tree-formed cerebellum and the divine tree of Diana. She read about the crystals that form in a tree struck by lightning.

She descended into the roots of the little words, like inconspicuous ants, each one carrying its stick, going from one meaning to another, from one branch of language to another. Words fluoresced in clusters of significance, burst open and floated hopefully in a kind of searching mood, scattered widely, indiscriminately, like rain, and indeterminately, like pollination, attaching to meanings like the legs of bees. From one to another she read, like going on a walk in an unfamiliar place, wandering from intensity to intensity.

"What word was I looking up again?"

Maya was startled out of her reminiscences by the sudden movement of a raven that had landed right next to her, so close she could admire the intricate filigree of its black feathers laid one against the other. The raven studied her in turn, then flew away. She picked up the guidebook and resumed her reading.

No one could ever solve the mystery of the seven sudden, blade-less beheadings of the seven heads of state, vanished without a trace in a cloud of improbability. A quick, exuberant flourishing characterized that legendary time when a general strike was followed by universal agreement to greenhouse gas abolition, the great turn towards an Indispensable Universal Elemental Providence, and the unstinting work of bio-spherical remediation, carbon sequestration, and planetary ceremonies of repair, conducted according to local customs, heritages, languages, dialects, and lineages on a continuum from newly crafted cultures to immemorial traditions. The seven empyrean flowers which appeared the week of the beheadings grew hundreds of meters in a matter of days. Who knew how tall they would grow, or if the growing would ever stop? But after that week they slowed to a meter or so a year until they finally reached 700 meters. Their miraculous gigantism was notable enough to make the news, and since in each instance they had exploded into their colorful glory in states where the seven recycled heads of state had once dysfunctioned, it was later thought that perhaps these were memorial plantings of some kind. There are any number of theories, but no one knows for sure.

But Maya *did* know why it was that in the very countries where the seven heads of state rolled, the flowers grew taller than the tallest buildings. She knew it was her own mother's artwork that had scripted, depicted, and simultaneously instantiated these beheadings, the seven sacrifices which helped the lifeworld to slither through the narrowest of bottlenecks and escape extinction. A final straw, a pipeline becoming a stem, the future at last arrived flowering into present time *for every second was a narrow gate through which the messiah could enter.*

Jane's had been a solitary, invisible, unstoried messianism, by means of an artwork years in the making, a psychokinetic animation she called *Seven Days of Decreation*. Her vanishment coincided with the first screening of it, a rendering of what Jane used to call *the end of the end*, followed by many beginnings.

Maya daydreamed under the great red flowers. Lambent red light moved across the café floor tracing the sun's descent. She looked out the immaculate windows and thought about cleaning the window and door frames of her cabin when she got home. Jane's face precipitated up out of the nowhere of thought, a memory of her scrubbing the doorjamb with tea tree oil to prevent mold. Angular, slight, sloped shoulders, muscular arms, and steel-toed boots. In the rainy season her skin was the hue of a faded page in a very old book, freckled faintly like the occasional rare eggshell. In the heat of fire and smoke season her skin turned the autumnal color of big leaf maple in October, its hand-like leaves piling up on the ground.

From being with Jane and seeing through her world-loving eyes she learned to perceive beauty. They would pause and point, show each other its poetry. Fog sloping downhill then unrolling low on the ground. Bales of hay set in the dirt like a message. A bell rung far away. A chair tipped back with legs and feet crossed on a table to balance. A cat sitting on a car. Incense smoke coiling. A neck craned to look at a crane. Undulating serpents of serpentine striated green in a sheer cliffside. Orange dress, the low hum of bees in lavender, shaking hands, strangers singing together in the streets, a sympathetic magic, the kairos of upwelling liberation movements, flickering shadows of swaying branches on the pages of a poem in which revelation undoes sentence . . . the shape of the everyday was never the same. Beauty appeared in flashes all around and between them, like a wave showing itself to the sea. This beauty moved everywhere; illuminated. Quotidian, exquisite, serviceable, kind: love was the greatest beauty of all. Its fabric ever more intricately patterned.

When Jane vanished, where went this admirable variation? Maya felt static, unreal, inanimate, indifferent to the changed moral fate of the world. Everything was better for everyone, justice and goodness flourished. But what was morality compared to love? *Love is the good life*, she thought. She had once imagined that love and morality were the same.

She distanced herself from everyone and everything. She practiced her own extinction. She was at her calmest when she could welcome death completely, with no confusion nor anguish. The ignorant apocalypse was over. Lying on the floor Maya imagined her body parts disappearing one by one until there was nothing left. Inert, lignified, she vanished too. When I *am* loss, she realized, there *is* no loss. To decompose was also to live, as loss, so that it no longer impended. This was how she rejoined Jane: nothingness joined to absence, *the distant turning toward the distant*, she crossed the diagonal of death.

The universe was a psyche, trying to find the source of its abandonment. The continents drifted uncertainly. She traveled this place that was a mind, in the vehicle of self as an instance of it. A self that didn't belong to her and that she would never fully understand.

Fabric was the metaphor that revealed space-time. Maya imagined a resplendently glowing blackness, an infinite rippling net stretching on forever, weighed down in places by planets and the other cosmic entities, in other ways defined by weightless abstractions such as constellations of divine animals, parables of heaven, stars as weightless as thoughts. They turned into stories that reenacted themselves forever until the sun burned down.

She once made a painting of death. It was a vast patched coat, of a piece even with all its torn parts. The sleeves were black holes, the buttons were planets. Their mass attracted anatomical-looking folds, circular avenues.

2.

Until she was six, Maya and Jane lived alone together in an apartment building in a foggy city. When she turned seven, they moved to a different neighborhood to live at the Anarchstery, a former convent inhabited by a collective of ex-nuns who had started a school and a farm. Then, at the beginning of Maya's third set of seven years, when she was fourteen, they moved again. Now they lived alone again, in a streetless forest where trees floated up to the sky, a place that was completely dark and quiet at night.

In the noisy, hot, bright, and spread-out city Jane's every thought had revolved around deteriorating social and climatological conditions and their political roots. Her perceptions and feelings were political: political depression, political fury, political desire, and political resolve. She had become increasingly convinced that general immiseration, domination, exploitation, and degradation were ultimately caused not just by the fact of, but the very concept of "world leaders" who distracted people utterly from world-making on their own terms. The world leaders were like a loud, incessant noise that made it difficult to think.

On the wall above the kitchen sink Jane had tacked a segment of an interview with Mike Davis given three months before his death. Maya had read the fragment while doing the dishes so many times, she knew it by heart. It concerned the question at the core of many arguments she had with her mother:

Bolsheviks were always opposed to individual acts of violence, because Russia had so much experience with that before the revolution—the Leninist argument was that you're substituting the heroic deed for mass action, the heroic sacrificial individual for the class. It made a lot of sense. To me political violence is something to be judged much more rationally than morally. And there are instances: After the death of Franco, the Francoist transition to preserve the regime had all been set in place. Carrero Blanco was the anointed successor to Franco, and a group blew his car over a cathedral. It totally disrupted the succession and made relative democratization possible. We know on the negative side that if Fanny Kaplan hadn't shot Lenin, Stalin might not have happened. To me it's an open question depending on context and conditions.

§

In those first seven years of Maya's life when they lived in the grey apartment building on a noisy four-laned street in the city, Maya tried to dissolve Jane's anger with gentleness, but it had become too hardened. Poor anger! So battered and beaten. How could Maya help? What could she do? She tried to comfort her mother, to reassure her. But Jane's painful feelings billowed out, pushing Maya away. For nothing was as it should be, the violence of the state was everywhere and yet nowhere.

When they saw people trying to sleep on the sidewalk with their arms over their eyes to block streetlights, little Maya asked why. Jane explained: *The earth and the star that lights our days invented sleep for us, with a loving black shadow of quiet, but industrialization destroyed darkness. So-called world leaders, usurpers of the sun, planet sickeners; they are the ones who deprive sleepers of night.*

Maya suffered a feeling of drowning in the air, as if locked out of the world. She gasped as she lost, hunted and thirsted for oxygen. She would have to leave the house or go into her room; she had to be alone to swim down below this internal vortex rather than flailing out of it only to be pulled deeper.

Children deafened by bombs, wiping their mother's blood from their faces . . . misdeed of states.

To swim under, until a lateral current came and pulled her out. Her failure to overcome her mother's anguish, which was the world's anguish, defined her.

Although they didn't own a television, for a period her mother listened to the speeches of those "leaders" who used the law to control other people's bodies while using the state to profit from weapons that killed the children they pretended to protect. She would listen to them in real time, threading her own incantations through their address.

What will happen when we act instead of pretending to act, we won't be dreamed by you any longer . . . I frame your neck in vivid red, see it now: you lose your head . . .

Sometimes, Maya remembered, it seemed as if Jane's incantations would cause the speaker to falter. Their speech would grow garbled, obscured by static the source of which no one could locate.

The angrier Jane was the more Maya struggled to breathe. She sat up straight, lifting her ribs, looking under them for precious caches of air. She lifted her arms, twisted her spine, moved her body around in strange positions, tried to be a more hospitable vessel for the air. Breath could be hiding anywhere, she just had to find it. The way she searched was by making shapes with her body, or sometimes jumping, dancing, or crawling until she found it, or it found her, only to to be lost again.

Lack of money was a chronic problem too. Jane waited in welfare lines and made her case with case workers. The welfare office was filled with tired people on long lines filling out endless forms. Maya stood next to her mother holding her hand and fantasized about finding treasure. In those desolate centuries, the anxiety all poor children had about money was soothed by stories of treasure hunting, a precursor to job hunting: there was more than enough money, it was just hidden. It was a matter of searching well. Sometimes it was found in other people's pockets, purses, wallets, or hidden in floors, walls, jars, attics, buried under trees. The point was to get some of the hoard, so little it wouldn't be noticed, yet enough that it could change everything, at least for the moment. The key was to not wake the dragon in the process (to not get caught.)

This was the child's training in the drive for surplus, how to sneak away with something. The capitalist simply killed the old dragon and took everything. The greatest treasure was its fossilized body. The dragon's body was burned to create countless versions of the disposable nonesuch, vast gyres of it suffocated silver scaled fish, made oceans into cages, pits. The children grew up and found work, which, no matter how useless or destructive, hid the thieving drive of capitalism. Being fired was getting burned while quitting was an unsung ecstasy, though it lasted only until the money ran out.

§

Maya couldn't remember anymore exactly how long it had taken them to travel from the city to the woods, whether it was three days or two weeks or several months to get to the disheveled bungalow that became her lifelong home. She did remember they arrived on a clear blue morning. She recalled feeling engulfed by trees, walking in the forest and watching beams of sun glimmer in the trees. Jane's mood improved and so, then, did Maya's. They savored the trees' scents on the air, the soil that smelled coppery with rain. They breathed sunlight as it jumped off the leaves. Breathing was different there, a respite. The narrow band around Maya's ribs gradually loosened. The breath she had been holding slid up between her spine and ribs until she felt a moist, clicking latch open in her sternum, a sweet turn, like a drink.

The bungalow in the forest was low-ceilinged and Jane, who was tall, tended to stoop, though there was a foot of clearance above her. It was an adjustment to move to this cave-like home which needed so much work. Dried nests and burrows of uncertain substance, little homes within the home, had to be dismantled and swept out.

The bungalow changed form over the years as they continuously repaired and experimented, as a way, among other things, for Jane to continue to educate her daughter in the political-philosophical implications of the practical arts. Maya remembered the pleasure she took in working side by side with her mother, clearing and cleaning, scrubbing and arranging, building and fixing, finding and making what they needed, improvising, studying their home together. It was, Jane said, their collaborative art project. She encouraged Maya to *dream the house*, to take notes on accidents of perception, mental projections, synchronicities, and unusual occurences as ideas to think with; material for the art they were making together. And so Maya began a list that grew for years until she no longer needed to write such things down, they simply stayed with her, her mind a book she could open to any page in time to remember a glimpse of four legs seeming to run, in low light, across an an old rippling wall; a beehive in a chipped window sill; a coalition of red robins, bluejays, and black crows harrying a grey, egg-thieving owl; a single bead of water gleaming like a diamond in a splashcup; a spherical spider web as large as a human head holding sticks, moss and leaves inside; the sight of a bear with an arrow partially buried in her shoulder, picking, with her good arm, wild apples with three cubs; dreaming the name of someone you've never met, and then meeting them the next day; many times of dreaming herself dead, traveling around in the afterworld, learning.

As they measured and cut, hammered and dug to expand the bungalow, Jane spoke about Euclidean transformations in geometry and changeable social structures, asking Maya to see where and how the story of their life, which they wrote with their actions, was inseparable from stories others had written, were writing, with their actions, which recreated the world every moment. "Move past thinking *about* form, and instead think *from* form," she encouraged her daughter. "Forms are everywhere, structuring and patterning experience."

They made one wall of hexagonal windows, and installed another wall with a herringbone pattern using extra shingles leftover from redoing the roof, bringing the outside in. They built a deck around a cedar hundreds of years old with a swerving trunk, a "leave" tree spared from logging because of its inconvenient sway, unconducive to milling, too wildly grained, giving a lesson in how to escape the predations of industry. Over the years the floor around the cedar sloped upwards as the tree added rings to itself, recording the movement of the earth around the sun, pushing outward incrementally, a faithful archivist.

The vegetable plots in the garden were visible from the kitchen sink. Behind the house was a cracked and fragmented cement pool, rectangular and long, which they repaired with salvaged tile and grout.

Jane swam up and down the length of the pool, somersaulted underwater, kicking off symmetrically without making a sound, lapping tirelessly. Maya liked to feel the softness of the water on her skin, to be lapped, to float on her back.

After Jane's disappearance Maya stopped cleaning or using the pool, and it was reclaimed by the forest, filled with leaves, dirt, ferns, sticks, and seedlings, small trees growing in it, until it was entirely hidden.

In Mesopotamia, Maya had read, houses were stacked like clay dishes on terraced hillsides continuously built up over generations. Under every generation, other generations. Under every age, other ages.

When Jane vanished their art project stopped. Notes that Jane had tacked to the wall of her study remained, faded to blank. A tree fell, knocking out the gutter and flashing they had put in together and cracking the small concrete patio; Maya didn't repair any of it.

The house waited. She waited.

To wait was to be on her way somewhere, but never just yet. She came to know waiting so well, how to hold her mind down. How to be still as a statue, soothe the nerves of discordance with the cells of impassivity. Long-lived organisms knew how to be still. She would learn from trees and turtles to leave things alone, not to try to figure it out, be inconspicuous, sometimes floating like a cloud, other times vibrating like a chord, other times becoming as heavily vast and radiant as a golden mountain.

After Jane's disappearance, the house, too, sensed the lack of her. Every object seemed to have forgotten its name and place, seemed to hover, asking, *Where*? Maya and the house waited for Jane to return, until waiting and life were one and the same.

On the perch of waiting, everything else disappeared into Jane's disappearance, until finally she did too. Jane became "____," an empty blazon. Meanwhile, it rained. Windows open, Maya would fall asleep inhaling rain. The house was being encroached upon by a ravine. She had a recurring dream that the house fell into it. She would wake from this dream in a torpor, the sky darkened by downpour.

She would ask the asymmetrical house out loud what to do about the erosion, following in her mother's footsteps, who used to talk to the house, ask it for advice. But when Maya tried to talk to the house, it acted depressed. *Go ask the rain*, the uneven house replied. *It isn't me but water that goes wherever it wants. And I only am, I can only be, I must only be starting from this strange, dislocated bearing of the infinitely other in me. I must carry the other, and carry you, the other must carry me . . . even where the world is no longer between us or beneath our feet, no longer ensuring mediation or reinforcing a foundation for us. I am alone with the other, alone to him and for him, only for you, that is, yours: without world. I am left with the immediacy of the abyss that engages me on behalf of the other wherever the "I must"— "I must carry you"—forever prevails over the "I am."*

Then it was silent, and Maya became invisible. Squirrels, snakes, salamanders, and birds ignored her as if she was a ghost. She could stand right next to deer, and they wouldn't run away.

Perhaps her life had ended, she'd died when her mother left, and this was her afterlife. Memories emerged out of the earth of the past, seeped like water. Memory was a painful companion.

3.

The collective Maya and Jane had lived in for seven years between their time when Maya was an infant, in the grey building in the grey city, and their life together when she was a teenager, in the artful bungalow, in the lacy green wood before Jane's vanishment, was a syncretic, breakaway convent with a windy old dining room, tall ceilings and windows, and spacious rooms. It was called The Anarchstery of the Rosas Parks and Luxemburg.

The buildings were airy; the stairs, doors, windows, and floors creaked. The rooms were spacious, open, and permeable. They had moved there at the invitation of the sisters, a collective of nuns—or as they liked to call themselves, variously, the "nouns," the "nones," "no ones," "noons," and "nines," though more usually the "Rosas," short for Sisters of Rosas — so that Jane could get help caring for Maya while she pursued studies in film, history, sociology, political economy, literature, and physics. The nuns ran a residential deconstruction company which Jane helped with, and a small elementary school. The Rosas helped care for Maya while Jane attended classes.

Dogs and cats also lived there, or at least were fed there, who came and went of their own accord. Some were more consistent than others. They were known by their looks and characters, but the nuns had not named them. Maya wanted to name them. One old German shepherd would occasionally be taken over by the desire to reenact his prior role as a guard dog, but he had no sense of who belonged and who didn't, as so many people came and went, sometimes staying for weeks or months, other times just for the night, trading a few hours of daily work for lodging. This dog would randomly just start barking at whoever was in the same room as him, *get out of here, get out!* He barked for a few minutes, and then, as if waking up from a dream, he brushed against the legs of whomever he had just been barking at and gave an apologetic look. Maya named this dog Crazy.

After Crazy got his name, he rarely barked any more. Maya and Crazy stuck together. Occasionally the aged dog would bark, just once. This high pitched, forceful shriek shattered anyone who happened to be nearby, though not Maya. Crazy's singular shriek rippled through her like a cloudburst, a silver crack of light.

On her desk in her small room at the Anarchstery (Maya and Jane's rooms were next to each other and connected by a door, with a shared sink) Jane had her old childhood copy of Vladimir Mayakovsky's *How Are Verses Made?* given to her by her mother, and dedicated to Jane by Mayakovsky, after whom Maya was named.

He had been a playwright, a poet, an artist, an actor, and a maker of children's books and posters. In *A Cloud in Trousers* the street is a character who "shoves pain along" and "coughs up its phlegm" while the poet proclaims his bodily mettle, his weather, he is "pure raging meat," a "sack of grisly meat," "made of bronze" with a "heart lined with iron," "not a man, but a cloud in trousers!" He did his cultural work, warned the angels, "winged fools" "I'll slit you" and threatened the Almighty ("a jerk") with a knife. "Heaven! Get that hat off! Here I come!" for "muscle and sinew work better than prayer" so "I'll rip out my soul / stamp on it / to make it big / and hand it to you / bloody for a flag."

"Wearing the thorny crown of revolution" he made public art to inculcate communist sensibilities during the Russian Civil War. But Mayakovsky was soon at odds with the revolutionary Russia he had helped write into being. He satirized it and was denounced in turn. Posthumously he was celebrated by his enemy, the tyrant Stalin.

Jane took to heart what Mayakovsky called the *social command*, the communist's vocation, an obedience to the people, to the many, to the desires and objectives of your class. The social command concerns a problem "the solution of which is conceivable only in poetical terms." Though she had never known the poet, she had been told by her Soviet mother Hannah that he was her "progenitor" as she put it in her typical impersonal way, from a single drunken night. Some time after he killed himself Hannah fled the country with her child. It took her years to get to Brooklyn only to die of asthma when Jane was still a teenager, leaving her to fend for herself.

Decades later Jane repeated her mother's style of begetting, getting pregnant from one night's sex with a much older man she never saw again, a wanderer, a stranger she met at a train station. He said he was a computer scientist and claimed to have invented the internet. He was voluble about the apocalypse and told her of a Mayan prophesy that the world would end. The Mayans, he said, called creation itself the Framer, the Shaper, and built galactic observatories to predict and represent the flows of time and the universe as an eternally changeful form.

"The Shape Master has abandoned us," he said. Her own intensity rose to greet his. She felt the same mad fear for the world. "The world will end soon," he said, and his eyes filled with tears. "My whole life there has been an apocalypse." She told him she thought the world was *not* ending soon, but rather it was going to begin again. "There is a future," she said, and she believed it. She *knew* it.

He was moved by Jane, and she felt desire for him despite his abjection. Or perhaps because of it. He was missing teeth but did not lack passion. Touching each other made them feel exquisite, endless and hopeful. Later, he told her his backpack had been stolen with all his money. She gave him most of the cash she had before getting off the train. He stayed on, going north to meet up with his agent, so he said. She believed he meant it, even though she knew it wasn't a fact. They couldn't wait to see each other again yet made no plan. She didn't know his last name, where he lived, how to find him.

A month later, despite his age and hers, she found herself pregnant. She had had four abortions over her lifetime but decided to keep this improbable baby. For three years, on their anniversary, she took the baby on the train they had been on the day they met, but she never saw him again.

She named her baby Maya in honor of the prophesy the old man had taught her, and after the Vedic term for illusion, and after Vladimir Mayakovsky, Maya's alleged grandfather and tutelary spirit.

The name told the child everything about who she was, where she was. Each Maya within the proper name Maya encountered another Maya that had nothing to do with the other, yet something occurred between the three that didn't occur within any one of the Mayas, a conversation outside and between each one of them, just as she lived outside and between other lives, in the strewn condition of the flying root, thrown, diasporic, seeking and never finding home. The proper name "Jane" held within it the genius of the begetting gene, not to mention the dedicated aspiration not to cause a single harm—the Jain nuns would wear masks so as not to accidentally inhale an insect, would gently sweep the ground in front of them, not to step on one.

Jane had been traveling when she encountered the older man. When she arrived at her destination in a coastal city in the western reaches of the global patriarchal empire, she went through her pregnancy, gave birth in the free, local general hospital's maternity ward, and raised her child, Maya, for the first seven years of the child's life. They had a two-room apartment in a large apartment building near the beach. For much of the year their grey building was encased in a matching grey fog so that it could sometimes disappear. It was surrounded by empty lots so that the building itself, between the lots and the fog that crossed every line, blurring the horizon, seemed to exist like an island without connection to the rest of reality except the weedy plants, dandelions, fennels, pampas, and myriad other self-cultivating grasses and stalks, which grew up out of crevices like the children who skateboarded, played ball games, and jumped rope in the afternoons and evenings, until parents called them in from windows of diluted light. Even their clothes and faces seemed smudged by the fog.

When Jane saw a sign on the bulletin board in the lobby of their apartment building offering room, board, and childcare in exchange for part-time handywork and gardening at the The Anarchstery of the Rosas Parks and Luxemburg, she immediately went there and inquired.

She found herself wandering in an old Spanish convent with a grand, high-ceilinged stucco church with wax tiled floors, surrounded by scattered houses with low, red tiled roofs and wide oak floors, long windows, and arched doorways. It took her some time to find anyone. She finally came upon someone sweeping the paths, who pointed her in the right direction. She found the sisters in a large kitchen, preparing lunch. They asked her questions while they cooked, handing her a cutting board and garlic. She told them about the various kinds of jobs she had held, the skills she had picked up. *I can repair anything*, she said, slicing the garlic quickly and efficiently.

In addition to recognizing her competency with a knife, during the interview the sisters also recognized Jane as a fellow witch because of the half crescent moon neck tattoo, as well as the tattoo on her arm which showed a human body with a bird's head and roots for feet, coiled and embracing. She and Maya joined the community. They made plans, ate cherries, and drank coffee. Enid Rosas, who conducted the interview, herself of island ancestry, her mother from Martinique, her father from Ireland, wanted to get to know Jane. Enid and Jane conversed about having a prismatic heritage, of near ancestors nonetheless planetarily far flung, of how much history they wove in their cells through this kinning across oceans, a meeting taking place in Maya's DNA between Odessan Russian Jewish socialists and the unknown old prophet on the train. Enid's parents had been anti-colonial poets of the "tidalectic." *It is as if the body leaps across the world, from one definition to the next*, Enid said, *stranding us together.* The strands of diasporic heritages intertwined and pulsed in blooded and oil-slicked currents that drifted this way and that. Class and category—scarring legacies of slave states, alienated labor, industry and Cartesian duality—mixed contingently with organized and spontaneous forms of resistance, pained liberation prayers, and songs that argued and longed for justice.

Jane and Maya moved in, and it was as if they had been away after a long absence, as if they had always been part of the community, and, for the community, as if a missing piece had fallen into place. *Everyone was happier*, which meant their presence was needed. Needed for what? Enid wasn't sure yet. This called for divination.

§

The no-ones had a practice of *pre-admiration* in which they admired in advance those they had not yet met. They had one central high-ceilinged structure with long, large windows and surrounded by tall plants that was set aside for chance, where they practiced what they called *a ministry of immanence*. They called it the community living room. Nothing was planned there. It was a place in which one was free to be no one, do nothing, ask for help, or just rest, assist with projects on the farm or in the school, take solace, get medicine or food. Whoever arrived was welcomed as the no-ones venerated solidarity as an ethos within which free thought, free association, free will, and free love could flourish. They made agreements but changed them when and as needed, holding seminars for as long as was necessary to work on practical and theoretical problems, distribute responsibilities, and enjoy ideas and projects.

If it weren't for their vestments and the fact that they lived at a convent, or that they meditated and prayed for hours a day and spent their versatile days ministering to needs in versatile ways, using their spiritual imaginations to alleviate suffering, introducing children to experiential learning, and co-creating the possibility of collective happiness, it wouldn't have seemed like a religious order at all, insofar as no one gave or received orders, insofar as such orders had historically entailed the merging of life with rules *a priori*. In the rainy season they laid out mats and bedding and the Anarchstery grew crowded with people of all ages and conditions seeking shelter from the cold.

Enid Rosas, a visionary who co-founded the convent, had been a psychoanalyst until an illness led her to give up her practice and become a contemplative, after which her symptoms abated. She focused instead on writing and social care. She wrote towards a metaphysics of social care, dialecticizing the order she appropriated, adapted, and co-deconstructed along Black feminist lines. She wrote a series of pamphlets deconstructing monotheism: *When the Heavens Ceased to Be Social*, *No One But an Old Nun*, *Little Orphan Anarchy*, and others. It was Enid who asked, *what genre are we living out?* Every genre is an organization of time. She proposed duration as their orientation to time as time-beings. Days and nights that phased like the sky between songs, anecdotes, revelations, projects, plans, study, light, and darkness.

Jane's main task was to de-nail wood and sort salvageable lumber from the painted or rotting beams. With the unsalvageable lumber, she made worm boxes and compost bins, an arbor, a sauna, a pergola. Now that she had help with raising her young daughter Maya, she also had more time for her own pursuits while Maya attended the nouns' small school. It soon became apparent that although Maya didn't know many of the things other children her age knew, by the same token she did know things even her teachers did not know. She expressed her knowledge by means of drawings and paintings. She declared that she *hated history and geography*, a source of tension with her baffled mother for whom nothing was more important. It seemed to Maya that all the suffering which convulsed her mother relentlessly could be found under the very same subjects.

She would defend the rights of the void, of timeless and spaceless zero, worldlessness. Enid recognized it. Back when Enid had a psychoanalytic practice, she would have called Maya's retreat a "death drive." Now she saw it as the child's attempt to make shelter out of what her mother ignored. What didn't count in

Jane's epistemology was the nothing out of which Maya would try to make something, groundlessness on which she tried to construe a place to stand.

Maya had seen films playing in Jane's eyes, and she wanted to know how an image forms in the eye. One elderly teacher, the wiry and wry Napoleon Rosas, Enid's half-brother had worked in a glass factory twelve hours a day before he came to live with the Rosas, whose last name he then adopted. Napoleon explained the multidimensionality of sight, the structure of the ocular globe, the iris, pupil, and retina, the inverted image received by rods and cones and transformed into electrical impulses, the nerves and the optic chiasma, thalamic projections and then the visual centers of the occipital lobes, the lens focusing light rays and projecting them onto the retina . . . and here Maya asked why it was that one could see the images of another person's thoughts in their eyes? Napoleon thought Maya was referring to the way one could know how someone was feeling by looking into their eyes and spoke of empathy, mirror neurons, and interbeing. But Maya did not feel satisfied with this response, as it did not explain why she had seen images moving across Jane's eyes, miniature films, why she could see there what Jane was imagining.

What Maya perceived in Jane's eyes only became more unclear after a public debate and discussion, led by Napoleon and Enid, which drew from Adorno's "Theses Against Occultism" and Benjamin's "On the Concept of History." Napoleon described the nature of, and called for, historical thought, warning against what he deemed the historian's agon, the recourse to prophesy, "the smiling of auguries," and he elaborated on what he called an *intimacy* between occultism and totalitarianism. He read from "Theses Against Occultism":

> *Superstition is knowledge, because it sees together the ciphers of destruction scattered on the social surface; it is folly, because in all its deathwish it still clings to illusions: expecting from the transfigured shape of society misplaced in the skies an answer that only a study of real society can give.*

Enid in her turn drew on Benjamin's conceptions of history to muse on the possibility that too much clarity could be a kind of madness, to say that historicism could never be entirely neutral, to propose that historical materialism should embrace its occulted theology: "Spiritual goods are also necessities." Perhaps, Maya thought, she had too much clarity about what Jane was imagining, the outlines of bodies without heads. It must not pertain to her, as Jane never spoke to her about it. Yet, why did she see it, if it didn't pertain to her?

The noons eschewed traditional habits. Instead, they made their own bright green, colorful vestments, patterned work aprons, and other garments worn in common to signify their commitment to communality, co-creation, and co-consecration.

Jane shook her head at these robes, their originality notwithstanding, their uniformity of display, as if you had to dress as someone special to do good works. Enid countered that finding and expressing sameness was better for communalism than fetishizing difference, that the investiture, the fabricated consecrations of rank, belonging, and commitment marked by the cloth, transformed the wearer into a walking temple. Our uniforms—unity of form—change from time to time, Enid pointed out, not to denote advancement, but to revel in style; to reveal it; to incorporate revelation: when a no-one had a remarkable insight what was seen was sewn into the seam, the fabric of life.

The noons had no mother superior. The pervasive figure of the "mother superior" had not been an alternative to patriarchal domination but had masked and normalized its hierarchical violence. The mother superior was a compensatory figural mother whose opposite number was the *mother inferior*: motherhood as the road to abjection and hunger, motherhood as a cause of poverty, disrespect, and isolation, sentimentally valorized by hypocritical churchmen.

The noons prayed and meditated individually and together, in a rhythm that seemed intuitive and changeable. They practiced collaborative lucid dreaming to solve problems and make decisions. They reversed the usual formula of dream interpretation in which the dream was first remembered and then explicated. They made interpretations first, and then had dreams out of their interpretations.

It was after one of their collaborative dreams that they called Jane in from the grounds where she was planting trees and asked her to meet with them. They had made an interpretation about Jane, and then set out to have a dream about her. In it she had been swimming with a group of sharks, carrying a candle underwater that somehow stayed lit! The sharks had allowed her to follow them. Holding her candle, Jane watched them hunt, shed thousands of teeth, and swim-sleep on the ocean floor. The candle flame turned into a leaf, the candle into a branch. As the sharks slept, rocking their bodies gently side to side, their bodies turned to great green leaves breathing and swaying, catching the light, their teeth were leaves, the ocean became a forest.

Enid offered the interpretation they wrote out before the dream: *one form becoming another.* Enid handwrote their interpretation for Jane on a piece of blue notepaper, which Jane folded up and kept in her wallet for the rest of her life.

Trappists made ale; the noons grew milk thistle to be planted where plutonium was being detoxified. They made oyster mushroom mats to soak up oil spills that suffocated water. They manufactured chlorella formulas for cancer patients. Under the tutelage of the dream, Jane began experimenting with chlorophyll as a medium. She made anthotype prints out of flowers. Chlorophyll, Jane learned, is a detoxifier which filters out xenobiotics—*strangers to life*—such as phytates, dioxins, pesticides. Reflecting green light in photosynthesis, or red light to dissipate heat and convert chemicals into vibrations, sloughing excess energy on a diet of ultraviolet, binding to mercury, lead, nickel, and aluminum like a wrestler, chlorophyll embraced and devoured that which destroyed life, offering death to death, on behalf of life.

§

Along with Crazy, Maya had made another friend when they first moved to the Anarchstery. At nine, Cassandra was two years older than Maya when they first met. Cassandra was being raised by her grandfather Napoleon. Napoleon and Cassandra lived in a passive solar house which he had built near the community living room. He taught in the school, cultivated roses, and played his trumpet.

Napoleon taught the children about his marauding namesake, Napoleon Bonaparte, how he had put all of France and its colonies in kinds of adaptable barracks after the French Revolution: barracks for science, theater, childcare, travelers, and so on, and these institutions had lasted centuries. Bonaparte colonized Napoleon Rosas' ancestral land of Martinique, where he and Enid's mother was originally from, and brought slavery back to the Caribbean in 1802 when he took power. It had been abolished in 1794. "Which goes to show us," Napoleon Rosas said, "that history is not linear, that we do not put the worst behind us, it does not stay locked in the cabinet of the past."

Napoleon taught them about the insurrection in Martinique in 1848, about the Caribbean poetry and philosophy that emerged from island consciousness, and from uprisings and decolonizations. He taught them about how the colonizers imported their practice of witch killing in Europe to the Caribbean and about the universality of resistance in the face of inquisitors, tyrants, conquererors, and dominators, when resistance is reason, sense-making itself.

Maya had never had so much fun in her life as she had with Cassandra. In retrospect, when she remembered their times together, she wondered if she had had fun at all before they had met. It didn't matter what they did: everything was fun. Whether making forts together, climbing pipes on the side of the main building to the roof, skipping rocks at the local lake, lying on their backs looking at clouds, reading quietly next to each other, playing cards, dress-up, hopscotch, basketball, checkers, or chess, talking about everything they felt and thought about, studying together, showing each other their drawings, walking around with Crazy, everything was fun.

Napoleon said to them one day, "I can see that you two are real friends, because you inspire each other. That's what friends do!" He then read aloud to them from *Discourse on Voluntary Servitude or the Anti-Dictator* written by Montaigne's closest friend, Étienne de la Boétie, when he was eighteen.

> *I should like merely to understand how it happens that so many men, so many villages, so many cities, so many nations, sometimes suffer under a single tyrant who has no other power than the power they give him; who is able to harm them only to the extent to which they have the willingness to bear with him; who could do them absolutely no injury unless they preferred to put up with him rather than contradict him. Surely a striking situation! Yet it is so common to see them bewitched and charmed by the only name of one . . .*

"Why does it happen?" Cassandra interrupted, "it's so stupid: I would never go along with it." Napoleon said, "Let's read on and see."

> *He who thus domineers over you has only two eyes, only two hands, only one body, no more than is possessed by the least among the infinite numbers dwelling in your cities; he has indeed nothing more than the power that you confer upon him to destroy you. Where has he acquired enough eyes to spy upon you, if you do not provide them yourselves?*

How can he have so many arms to beat you with, if he does not borrow them from you? The feet that trample down your cities, where does he get them if they are not your own? How does he have any power over you except through you? What could he do to you if you yourselves did not connive with the thief who plunders you, if you were not the accomplice of the murderer who kills you, if you were not traitors to yourselves?

"Now, what is he saying?" Napoleon asked.

Cassandra replied, "He is saying that the tyrant's body is made up of everyone's body, that *he literally is the world and not at all a person*."

Maya felt tension building in her body. The iron band that constricted her breathing was back. *I hate history*, she thought, and wondered where the thought came from. *I hate subjects and topics* her mind went next. *They aren't people.* This conversation was just like her mother when she was at her most distant and unreachable. When she was like a hallway, full of entrances and exits, with nowhere to sit. Maya sensed that there was a need in the world for something Jane could provide, a need for her to provide it, no matter the cost to Maya whose own position was perpetually ambiguous. She felt trapped: trapped by this description of things, unequal to the flat sizes of history and geography, which were there and not there, trapped in her bulbous and indefinite body. She stared at a camera sitting on a shelf. Moveless, it presented itself. She fidgeted, stroked Crazy's rustled leafy back, and wanted to leave. She said, "If the tyrant is the world, and we live in the world, how can we get away from him? How can we get away from the whole world."

"Let's read on and see," Napoleon said. He read on.

I do not ask that you place hands upon the tyrant to topple him over, but simply that you support him no longer; then you will behold him, like a great Colossus whose pedestal has been pulled away, fall of his own weight and break into pieces.

There are always a few . . . who feel the weight of the yoke and cannot restrain themselves from attempting to shake it off . . . They cannot prevent themselves from . . . remembering their ancestors and their former ways. These are in fact those who, possessed of clear minds and far-sighted spirits, are not satisfied . . . to see only what is at their feet but rather look about them, behind and before, and even recall the things of the past in order to judge those of the future . . .

"Like Enid," Maya said. "And like Jane," Cassandra said. "Yes," Napoleon, "like them, and anyone, including you, who can remember . . ."

For three years Cassandra was Maya's whole happiness, her world. They witnessed Crazy's death together, burying him, making a shrine to him, and holding a memorial with other dogs and cats in attendance. Maya's learning and growing took place inside that frictionless world of Cassandra and Crazy. Then, at age thirteen, Cassandra began to change, and Maya and Cassandra's relationship also began to change. Now Cassandra wanted to go by Cass. Cass wanted to know more about history, geography, freedom, about the conditions of the past and the potential of the future. Cass was developing political feelings, political desire. The wounds of history hurt. She wanted to know: what is the antidote?

Maya just wanted to keep playing together and having fun. She didn't want to think about all the things that Jane and Enid, and now Cass, wanted to think about, the suffering in the world, and how to heal it; oppression and how to liberate it; how to begin again at the end of the world. Sometimes when Maya and Cass were together, and Cass began to talk about the horror of history, including Cass's own ancestors' experiences of enslavement in the Caribbean, Maya turned up a sound inside her head to drown it out.

The sound got louder and louder on its own, until one day she found she could not turn it off. All day and all night she heard this sound. Sometimes it comforted her, and other times it tormented her.

Cass began to spend time with other teenagers and started smoking. Cass never wanted to play anymore, only watch films Maya couldn't understand, read books Maya couldn't understand, write poems Maya couldn't understand, and talk about things that made Maya sad. Maya was alone, with the sound. After dinner one night Maya asked Cass to play chess. Cass said no. Maya asked, "Why?" Cass said, "Because you don't listen to me. You pretend to listen to me, but you ignore me."

Maya flushed. She walked away, thinking but not saying, *You're the one who ignores me*. She went outside and walked aimlessly, not recognizing her surroundings, not knowing where she was going, until she saw an enormous willow tree. She crept under low curtaining branches that swept the ground, leaned against the trunk and cried. Then she lay down on her back. She heard the sound in her ears and thought, *the sound helps me to ignore things. But what will help me to ignore the sound?* She began counting the leaves of the willow tree and soon the sound went away, or she forgot about it.

Her loneliness reemerged when the sound disappeared. It seemed to overflow like water searching for a limit, as if there was more of her than there used to be, all out of place. She needed to cut it off or pull it in. She pushed herself into the ground and then started covering herself with handfuls of soil.

§

Enid had introduced Napoleon to the British child psychologist D.W. Winnicott, his theory of transitional objects, transitional spaces, and holding environments. Napoleon was inspired. He developed a concept for a transitional object that would dissolve money. The exhange of art would replace the exchange of currency.

He guided the children in creating transitional objects out of all kinds of materials. Napoleon's idea was that these transitional objects would form the basis for a barter system in which all forms of labor would be equally valued. Each transitional object would be commissioned—based on conversations—and distinct. Each one different from the last—metonymic of the nature of the exchange. They could in principle be so elaborate and interesting, so emotionally important to their recipients, that they might take the place entirely of whatever barter they were created for, countering the contagious fetish of abstract value. To create a transitional object for someone, you needed to get to know each other, spend time together. Material objects and processes conceived primarily in terms of art, relationship, and gift, was how play and intimacy would inoculate against greed and acquisitiveness.

Napoleon told the children, "Marx said money is a social relation disguised as a metal, way back when money was made from mined minerals. *Mine*," he quipped.

"Currencies represented numeral values and were designed to portray the ostensible heros and values of whatever nation-state they hailed from, be it imperial Rome or post-colonial Zambia. But eventually, money just represented *lack*."

Napoleon and the other teachers left the students free to build out additions to their curriculum using the materials at hand. What engendered learning, they believed, was not the didactic method found in compulsory education, but rather a form of discourse known as *maieutikós*, or midwifing, in which the students' concealed and implicit beliefs are birthed into the open air, where they could be examined.

They learned variously about irregular geometry, anti-essentialist biology, undefined time, psychogeography, cosmic perspectivalism, Indigenous bioethics, comparative prophesy, Carribean history and poetry, animist surveying, landlocked dialectics, island tidalectics, premodern crafts, blind contour drawing, abstract painting, the agape of botany, guerilla acrobatics, post-human veterinary medicine, cooperative political economies, interspecies choreography, psychedelic physics, bird aesthetics, critical seance atavism, direct action embodiment, mixing space with mind, late night meditation, kincentric dance, maximalist stillness and minimalist activity, the telepathic archaeology of feminist home economics, agnotology, mathematics for architecture, aporia, and the contemplation of Not Knowing (not to be confused with ignorance).

They were also preoccupied with surviving and understanding the heatwaves, floods, extinctions, scarcities, and fires of everyday life, biospheric dysregulation, anxiety and depression knotted to "market deregulation," a code of loneliness.

The very elements: ingredients of life and death. "Fire and water determine us," Enid said. "Loss of homeostasis has always been the sign of dying . . . fire and heat spread, the water element dries up, which in turn depletes the earth element . . . the stars draw our eyes and admiration, their luminosity is real to us, though they are long gone . . ."

One day Enid lit a candle, and the community watched it flicker as she spoke.

A flame is limited, she said, *it doesn't spread unstoppably. Wisdom is characterized by the knowledge of how to contain, ritualize, co-regulate, organize, temper. The fires will not go out until their ideological source is extinguished, which will be as impossible as keeping a flame lit underwater.*

§

The children received instruction from Enid on how to travel without moving. They walked in silence, carrying pillows and blankets, to a patch of forest ten minutes away from the convent. Under oak and manzanita, they each took a seat. They sat in silence for several hours, with occasional breaks, listening. After a while Maya felt her consciousness in the tree canopy. She could feel her awareness in the leaves of the trees. She easily traveled, in and through her awareness, into the trees, wandering under rosy shadows where Napoleon's circled garden grew.

The brain seemed to have grown its axons and neurons in imitation of the trees, following their form. Up from the pituitary grew a stem and petals, opening and opening continuously. She felt that so many of the struggles of humanity had to do with the evolutionary stage of this moment.

Maya thought: *I'm waiting. We're all waiting, as if this whole world is some sort of waiting room.* She felt impatient and bored. She got up and quietly wandered away. She chanced upon a turkey with two chicks making high-pitched and plaintive chirps as if, Maya thought, to make sure they weren't left behind, *We're here, we're here, over here!* The parent turkey, so large compared to them, crunching through the grasses, seemed at once tentative and sure of herself. The sound of the turkeys as they disappeared in the grass rustled inside Maya. She saw yellow cloudbursts and she suddenly felt inseparable from that sound; she was the sound the birds made as they rustled. A glimmer of joy shone through her body, a pure and simple happiness she had never felt, this moment of becoming sound. After that she wanted to be outside as much as possible, listening to animals, so she could become sound again, and feel herself pervaded by its light and color.

That night at dinner, Maya and Jane sat at a table with three oldest of the nouns. Maya, in her heightened state, was enthralled. She wanted to talk with Cass or Jane, but they were at the other end of the table. They were discussing a book by Simone Weil,

On the Abolition of All Political Parties. They talked about making the transition from elected authority to entrusted wisdom and egalitarian collective action and lamented the superficiality of politics reduced to mere party ties.

Maya listened and looked out the windows at the changing light, as ephemeral as the shadows. Her elation began to subside. The objects outside sank away into indistinction transformed into an indigo sky, the branches of trees like black etchings on a sphere of dark blue glass.

Maya wondered out loud if trees go to sleep, if night is a relief to them, or if they waited for the sun, were eager for it? Enid said, "They live their lives, just as we do, first in the sun's light and then in earth's shadow. Like us, they have evolved in companionship with these alternations of light and season."

§

Jane worked every night at her desk at the Anarchstery, trying to uncover a pattern, to render visible a morphology of revolution as it crackled and struck like lightning. Orders, ladders, pyramids, knots, and great chains of being were facile, over determined. She tried to perceive assemblies, vortexes, bewilderments, ripples and the nighttime of intersubjective becoming.

She tried to hear and obey the social command, the intelligence of liberatory desire, its objectives, but for a long time she could not understand what it said. She felt in her own body the same impasse her species was caught in, the historical present as *block*, a cold high border wall of impossibility. The lack of *genres for transition*. The incessant noise of work work work, of business and busyness, and the numbing pervasion of violence made it difficult to discern the social command. She heard angry shouts, exhausted moans, the small fast drum of frightened heartbeats seeking relief and pleasure in the inane products of industrialisms that wasted the lands and waters.

At the Anarchstery, where silence was palpable, something you could touch, something you could be held by, she finally began to hear the music of terror, ordinary sorrow, and anger.

She heard:

No! We don't consent to extinction, in obeisance to states!

She understood it . . . the given world, which was a taken world, could not be accepted as it was . . . obedience to despair . . . it amounted to a form of superstition . . .

The social commended her to emptiness. Recede as much as possible into anonymity, it said. Give up her own name, disappear into world-historical action. Go on unknown. Study the broken mind of oppression, how to destroy it. Be the opposite of that despot that must replicate itself endlessly in other minds, colonizing and cancerous and *strike it down*. Strike!

Her study of tyranny had led her to thinking about tyrannical *atmospheres*: political, affective, and climatological, which in turn caused her to begin to read about fulminology, the science of lightning.

She did not merely want to understand the pathology of domination, but to find a medicine by which to eradicate and prevent it. Political neuroscience had constructed the concept of neural ideology and linked ideological tendencies to religio-carceral introjections of the proverbial "all seeing eye." She began to discern paradoxical, perverse imbrication between the desire to surveil and control while remaining (anti-socially) ethically screened, unaccountable.

Michel Foucault had explicated the function of the panopticon in which "a real subjection is born mechanically from a fictitious relation." The panopticon's central tower can be empty and still have its effect. The panopticon allowed one imaginary "I" to *over see* the compound eye, the multitude. Each real "I" was subject to that projection, seeing itself as other, through an empty gaze. Nobody was there, always watching.

The adverb, *mechanically*, was of great interest to Jane. On the one hand, to behave obediently because of imagined surveillance, was to behave *mechanically*: automatically. On the other, fiction was a machine. A machine that produced kinds of subjectivity.

Jane thought of how in *The Odyssey* the one-eyed cyclops, Polyphemous, whose name means *many-voiced*, was sabotaged by Odysseus the protean, who became Nobody to escape the one eye. Nobody could never be caught. Nobody got away.

The proliferation of fiction in every form, stories consumed by the millions had created a fictophilic culture. The tyrants of the day were pathologically enamored of fiction, especially their own. To promulgate images of themselves everywhere was their core ambition. Physically invulnerable in their guarded fortresses, they were nonetheless vulnerable in the battlefield of the imaginary. This was where Jane turned her artistic and scholarly focus—to aesthetic, bioenergetic, and somatic antidotes to tyrant consciousness.

She planned to offer to the world-imaginary—if only to its

unconscious, its collective dream life—an undoing, a simple de-creation story. Another seven days towards a world in which nothing is squandered, not even war-profiteering heads of state: they too would contribute to the world-garden with their minerality. After all, she reasoned, trees give nourishment to each other when it is needed, they decrease their intake of nutrients and water to send it to others. Humankind need not be less intelligent than trees, at least in that sense, despite being the 380 million years younger sibling of the arbor.

In a notebook later found and read by Enid and Maya, Jane characterized her project as a time machine with which to administer historical homeopathy.

How many times has someone wished for a time machine in which to go back and undo so-and-so's birth, to prevent genocides, invasions, massacres, and yet we fail to seize the opportunity to undo those who immiserate the masses and destroy the biosphere right in front of our eyes, right now? Whatever action we believe they, the ancestors, should have taken to prevent their catastrophe, those are the very actions we should take. We are always in the time machine. We don't need to go back. I will release that favorable toxin, a homeopathic dose of de-creation.

Projection as a cinematic act, as a psychological reflex, and as ideology entailed imagining others (always automatically, mechanically, without willing it). Could there be projection without a mind behind it? There had to be no one to blame, no one to point to, no one to catch, *unaccountable*.

The Great Turning had to be helped along by thoughts without thinkers, Jane realized: acts without actors. The real would emerge from the fictive, as it always did. The fictive would emerge from the real, as it always did.

§

The no-ones encouraged Jane to enroll at the local public university and she did. After earning an undergraduate degree (the oldest person in all her classes), she embarked on graduate studies on a fellowship which entailed teaching. She was thrown into the classroom without guidance, as if being a student was all the preparation needed. She had to give lectures. She wasn't sure how. Was it just thinking out loud?

She observed what other teachers wore and imitated them, put on button-down shirts and shiny shoes that clicked, pouring herself into the mold. She put away her old work boots. She dressed for a job in which she would assign reading, write on a chalkboard, and think out loud. This was class mobility, or just another loose end to organize oneself around, for a time, becoming a particle of a bigger whole, and participating in the mores of the institution.

Here, clothes signified very differently than at the Anarchstery, where garments signified the harmonization of individuality with collectivity, abolishing the impositions of class. At her new job, to dress *up*, to wear the proverbial white collar, was to ascend, to acquire the vestments of the non-working class. To live "the life of the mind" was to escape the life of the calloused hands, the life of the swollen feet, the life of the aching back, the life of the body dismembered, as in so many creation myths.

In the Babylonian creation story Tiamat's parts were strewn. The strewn continents reflected her sacrifice. The creation of the world was a dismemberment. Its decreation would also be.

When she was still a new teacher, her confidence, pride, and absorption in her project propelled her along. But as time went on, she got lost in thought, or pain, or weariness, and the students did too.

She would pose not one or two, but sometimes twenty or thirty questions in one lecture, one after the other, and students didn't know which part they should remember. Wasn't learning a kind of eating? Where was the morsel, the kernel? Her lectures were like trying to breathe underwater. *What is the point?* they wondered. One day she said, "I've got a point for you." She began with a passage from Marx:

> *Luther removed the servitude of devotion by replacing it with the servitude of conviction. He destroyed faith in authority by restoring the authority of faith. He turned priests into laymen by turning laymen into priests. He liberated man from exterior religiosity by making man's inner conscience religious. He emancipated the body from chains by enchaining the heart. But even though Protestantism was not the true solution, it formulated the problem rightly. The question was now no longer the battle of the layman with the exterior priest, it was the battle with their own interior priest, their priestly nature.*

She elaborated: "The 'servitude of conviction' caused mystification and enabled tyranny since those in its grip lost their own chisel of thought. They confused obedience with goodness."

"What is the difference," she asked, "between the servitude of conviction, the interior priest, the priestly nature, and goodness, that is, having a conscience? What is conscience? Is conscience a feature of language? A limb of the organism? An earthly element? Could we see conflict as always, when it came down to it, something to do with the vibrational, holistic, geometric science of conscience? On the one hand a wish for, an appeal to conscience, on the other a rejection of it? If one's conscience is diminished or numbed, why? If it is elevated and grounded, why?"

At the Anarchstery, every month the role of Altar Maker rotated, tasked to create and maintain it. Jane had noticed that Altar Maker, whomever they were, no matter what they were usually like, tended to be more cheerful and less enclosed in self-concern. To go as Altar Maker seemed to impart a way of being. Was the inculcation of conscience a matter of changing roles? It seemed the no-ones thought so. Fixed positions of any kind were rare. No one had the authority to determine anyone's schedule, which was decided upon by treating collectivity and autonomy as sentient, wedded equals. The tempos of daily life were decided upon together and altered as needed.

"When science is used to run society as a casino," Jane continued, "can conscience make any difference? Can it even survive? When society is gamed win or lose," she went on, "the true nature of contingency and probability, of indeterminacy and uncertainty, is misunderstood and obscured, as people resign themselves to living in a house of fake chance, in which 'the house' (the propertied) will always win, and in which the occasional ordinary person, in a reversal of ancient traditions of sacrifice, is confettied with random riches on no basis at all, at the cost of everyone else.

"Whereas for most of human history the whole—*peoples*—was inseparable from the part—*person*—now individual choices were held to be *more important* than the whole. Whereas individuals had sacrificed themselves on behalf of the whole, *now the whole is sacrificed for the individual.*

"Whole species desecrated, the whole animal world debased, tortured, which so-called 'human beings' could only do by making an ontology of brutality. Shadowlands of capitalist positivism, in which the torture and destruction of animals, the brutalization of all beings, is no matter of conscience, of love, of spirit, but of consumer choice, the domain in which we supposedly exercise our subjective 'values.'"

A student raised her hand. Jane asked if she could wait until the end of the lecture for questions. The student said the question couldn't wait.

"OK," Jane said, "if it can't wait . . . please, go ahead."

"Which of those points is the point again?"

Another student asked, suddenly, "Is what you are saying factual? I mean, how do we know if what you are saying is real or if you just made it up?" Another student said, "Are you saying luck is bad?"

Jane was embarrassed. The gap between what she was capable of and what they needed was baffling. She thought of quitting right then. But to continue her own project, she persevered.

A few students were undergoing metamorphoses. Others, needing rest, shelter, cures, were withdrawn, tired, folded inward, sometimes asleep. Sometimes they daydreamed or looked out the window. A few listened to music on their headphones, whispered to each other, or doodled. One day, a student stood up and pointed. Everyone stood and turned to look, surprised to see a red-tailed hawk sitting on top of a streetlamp outside the window. The hawk looked back with a kind of motivated interest as if it wanted to tell them something but wasn't at liberty to do so.

Jane walked in just as it flew away. They sat down and opened their books.

"Let's pick up where we left off," Jane said.

"The masters of suspicion," Jane began, "posited an imaginary world in which imaginary worlds don't exist."

She read aloud a passage in *The Future of an Illusion* as students followed in their books: "When St. Boniface cut down the tree that was venerated as sacred by the Saxons, the bystanders expected some fearful event to follow upon the sacrilege. But nothing happened, and the Saxons accepted baptism."

She placed the book down and leaned on the table with both hands. "But Freud is wrong, of course. *Of course,* something happened when St. Boniface cut down the sacred tree," she raised her voice, "it just didn't happen right away. They should have waited a little longer. The Saxons were right to fear the cutting of the sacred tree. When they gave up their sacred tree, they became contaminated with the saint's arrogance and it became thinkable for them to go all over the world cutting everyone's sacred trees, reducing all trees to one crucifixion. St. Boniface was wrong and so were they to accept it. The catastrophe of the cutting of sacred trees redounds on their descendants and, eventually, on everyone."

But the students, like so many others, exhausted by despair, had become resigned to clearcutting, accustomed to oil fires and climate floods, inured to the "forever wars" and the proletarianization of animals, habitats, oceans, even space itself, and were unresponsive, looking down, away.

So, Jane gave up on the rest of her lesson plan. Instead, she asked students to imagine they were not themselves but some other creature or phenomenon, something winged perhaps, or tiny, an ant for instance, or woodpecker. A whale, rain, or a mountain. They wrote and talked about this instead.

She began to ignore assessments, homework, tests. She eschewed lectures. Instead, they mixed their bodies with space. In pairs they made spontaneous shapes and movements with their bodies and mirrored each other's gestures. They felt space between each other grow palpably thicker when they moved closer to each other, and then thin as they moved away, the air becoming malleable material, an invisible clay.

They read aloud from books that interested them, played music, slept, talked, or drew pictures in their notebooks, developed their own aesthetic and political experiments, tried out prophesy, remote viewing, shape-shifting, wrote and performed plays, went for walks studying malls and botany, roads, clouds, trees, the making of pattern, the tracing of linkage, the endless surprise of fractality. They learned the difference between the plantation forest with its singular telos of producing maximum board feet, and the kaleidoscopic boreal forest upon which countless organisms rely, and which nourishes the earth as well as the sky. They learned that when the CIA decommissioned their remote viewing program in 1995 it expanded into the private sector. They practiced their own remote viewing drawings, focusing on finding out where elder trees were in danger.

Some drawings led them nowhere. They were analogies, not maps. Others led them right to mother trees. The question was, how to protect the tree against the axe? A few made plans to climb the trees at night like jaguars and tend old wounds made in the bark. These several disappeared into the forest.

She had stopped using the assigned textbook, which chopped knowledge up into bits. It looked like a menu, with pre-formed places for each dish. Here was the main concept, with a side of syllogisms and a dialectical drink, followed by the hermeneutic dessert, the tautological Special of the Day up on the blackboard. The idea was to serve knowledge up on a platter, measuring it, cutting it up, plating it, and serving it to diners whose palates had been estranged. She was expected to make her students eat everything on their plates then regurgitate what she had dished out. Their indifference to the curriculum was a more effective refutation than any pedagogical argument.

Maya had been given the *Popol Vuh* by Cass as a gift. She showed it to Jane, who had never read, seen, or heard of it. Jane read a section of it to her class– "The Defeat of the Lords of Xibalba."

Now, it was the lords' desire
To abandon their hearts to the dance
Of Hunahpú and Xbalanqué
Then came the words
Of One Death and Seven Death.

"Do it to us! Sacrifice us!
Do it the same way, at last!"

cried One Death and Seven Death
to Hunahpú and Xbalanqué.

"Very well.
Surely you will be revived.
What is death to death itself?

We are only here to gladden you,
As well as your servants and minions,"
said the twins to the lords.

The first to be sacrificed
was the very head of the lords
One Death by name, Lord of Xibalba.

So now he was dead, this One Death,
and then they took Seven Death,
and neither one came back to life.

All the Xibalbans
leapt to their feet and fled

once they saw their lords
were dead and being torn open,

their hearts ripped from their chests
as punishment for all they'd done.

The first lord was executed
straightaway and not revived,

but the other lord began to grovel
and weep before the dancers, unable
to accept the place he'd found himself:

"Pity me," he said, too late.

"Sacrificing kings kept the seasons turning," Jane said. "There was prescience in this idea: *the continuation of the seasons depended upon sacrificed rulers.* This was essentially an agricultural practice. The head that wore the crown was given to the earth, as a seed of social renewal, against the putrefaction of power. Symbolically and politically, the death of the ruler prevented the death of the world."

Abandoning the system had consequences she had not noticed at first. A few students had complained that she wasn't using the required textbook. Others disappeared. One student, Ovie, had a habit of leaving during the break and not returning. Jane would see Ovie outside, during class, lying on the grass, or talking avidly, quietly, intensely, absent-mindedly, irritatedly, variously with anyone who happened by. One morning just before class Ovie asked, "Am I going to fail?"

"No," Jane said.

"I'm sorry I missed so much class," Ovie said.

"What did you miss?"

"I don't know."

"Why do you leave class?"

"Maybe low blood sugar. Or because I don't want to be a believer."

"A believer in what?"

"In anything."

"I understand."

"How can I learn without being trapped in belief?"

"Is belief always a trap?"

"For me it's always a trap."

"You're free then? You're not trapped?"

"No. I'm trapped in disbelief, but I prefer it to belief."

"Study that then."

"Study disbelief?"

"Study skepticism; study negation; study refutation."

"Study opposition?"

"Or study opposites . . ."

"What is an opposite?"

"Something inescapably under, above, in front, or behind. Past participle of *opponnere*, an opposite gives us a same. You, opposite belief, for example, provide believers a side."

At that moment her supervisor walked in. Her supervisor asked her what they were reading. Jane held up her red copy of the *Popol Vuh* and told her they were reading a sacred book of Mayan culture, a verse translation of a prophetic K'iche' text of the midwestern highlands of Guatemala that her daughter gave her. The supervisor reminded her she had to lecture and stick with the textbook and use its study questions.

"Why aren't you giving lectures?"

"Do my words turn into their knowledge?"

"Of course! How else are we supposed to escape the morass of incomprehension, except by hearing smart people and learning facts from textbooks?"

"But what happens after they get home? Do they 'punch out' from thinking because we've acted as though it's merely a job? Anyway, the *Popol Vuh*, with its depictions of civil services and political warfare, is as much a study of political philosophy as our textbook."

"Students should be working on the discussion questions in the textbook."

"They're too removed from us. We can ask our own questions. We need to construct our problems for ourselves."

"But it's required," her supervisor replied. "What's your issue with it?"

"The textbook gives students the illusion that knowledge appears out of nowhere, that it isn't invented, labored over."

"It's how students learn about the great ideas."

"But all out of context," Jane said. "We want to read the primary texts."

"Those are difficult," the supervisor replied.

Jane said, "Things are difficult; that is why we study. Isn't difficulty the point?"

"Not at all," the supervisor replied, "retention is the point."

§

The supervisor would sit in on one of Jane's lectures the following week. She had not lectured in some time, had abandoned lectures along with the textbook. Of course, her job required public speaking, of which some are said to be more afraid than bombs, earthquakes, and predators. She was used to public speaking, but the idea of the supervisor's presence made her tense. What choice did she have?

The supervisor left. Jane and Ovie, the student of disbelief, left the classroom and began to walk around campus, meandering and talking. Ovie asked, "Is the assigned textbook the opposite of the *Popol Vuh*?" To which Jane asked, in turn, "Are prophesy and didactics opposites? Or are they just differently oriented to time, as methods of instruction? One being reproductive, the other subjunctive . . ." The student looked curiously at Jane, who walked awkwardly as if her knee hurt, and it did. "To oppose is to mobilize," Jane remarked, "it is to find causes. But opposites are not limited to two points, as you might think from the formal structure of a debate, or from the crucifixion which, at first, looks like a place where opposites meet, affixed to a moment in time, a symbol of reconciliation as sacrifice. If you scale up, the contexts for opposites and oppositions get complex. A line between two points attracts other lines. Soon there is a square, then a cube, then four-dimensional hypercubes—tesseracts . . ."

They talked and walked in very slow circles, passing the same groundskeeper, heavy entryways, pillars, a bronze dome, dismembered statuary, and all the time people whose different aspects caught changes in the light, reaching for possibilities, going this way and that. One with two gold front teeth, a dyed blonde crewcut, and a cat-faced backpack walking with someone in a charcoal grey pantsuit with glossy, swinging hair. Another with long extensions, peacock feather earrings, alligator shoes, and leather pants, thinking about the cabinet she was building. A trio wearing shorts and tee shirts with the same insignias, team members pondering the phenomenological reduction. A hungover barista studying corvids who was just then wondering what the word "animal" did to animals. A retired dancer writing an ethnography of techno-capitalism, a book of moving lines that would not stop writing itself. A hairless poet with an ocular migraine who had written that morning *the hole / in the noun*. A touchy geologist with sore vocal cords. A veteran in a wheelchair studying public health and trumpet. They walked and talked, after which Ovie continued to write nothing and miss classes.

Anticipating her supervisor's visit, Jane's tongue was tense. It felt larger than usual, as if it no longer fit in her mouth. Like a restless dog, it wouldn't nestle down. She felt compelled to bite it. Her eyes twitched. She couldn't sleep because she couldn't figure out where her jaw should be. It felt out of place. It seemed lost, as if it belonged to a different person.

On the morning the supervisor came to observe, Jane stood at the lectern and made a *hunh* sound, then coughed. A long silence followed. She squinted with her hands clasped behind her back. She pawed her notes and tilted her head. Her hands visibly shook. Her uncertainty and the conspicuous presence of the supervisor made an atmosphere. Students rustled, alerted by Jane's demeanor to the presence of threat.

Jane inhaled and filled her lungs like a diver. She forced herself to speak, the words careering up before her eyes as she peeled them off the page with her voice, not wanting to look up at anyone.

She began . . .

. . . but they could barely hear her low, hesitant, and plaintive voice. It was so faint, as if echoing from the far end of a long tunnel.

Her parts felt disconnected. She felt as if she was in several naked pieces, distributed around the slatted racks of a refrigerator. Where was her tongue? Now it slept in the back of her mouth like a skinless baby rabbit.

She felt her spirit, a spark, float out of her head and drift towards the ceiling. Without the spark of spirit, the sloshy lobes and sockets of innards subtly ordered by weights, tides, and planes, start to lose definition and purpose. She tried to coax it, to herd it back. She pointed with her mind. But influencing the little spark was like trying to catch light in your hand. She closed her eyes and said to the spark, *Come back!* She pictured the spark floating down. At that it seemed to perch on her head like a moth on a windowsill. In her mind's eye, it spiraled up and then down, back into her head.

She suddenly remembered a line from Rosa Luxemburg's *The Russian Revolution* that she had thought about for a long time when she first read it in her twenties: *The only way to a rebirth is the school of public life itself.* And now she knew what to do. She would address the supervisor directly with her remarks, not only as a representative of the institution but as an influential member of the public. She wouldn't set the supervisor above, outside, and beyond her pedagogy, but teach the institution. Rather than showing herself like a specimen, she would use the opportunity to *exert influence*. Jane looked out and met the supervisor's eyes. She abandoned the prepared lecture and spoke directly to the institution (in the person of the supervisor).

Her voice rang out confidently. Waves of ideation flowed into the ears and eyes of the institutional head—

> . . . regarding the way in which discursive practices produce what they think they only describe as if description comes after, this is an assumption which fails to incorporate the observer effect, on the other hand we must guard against an 'over-estimation of psychic processes' which Freud described as the cause of the invention of religion, an overestimation in which the neurotic, an 'animistic soul' is prey to the belief that she 'can change the outer world by a mere thought' and where the spirit's 'flightiness and mobility, its faculty of leaving the body, of permanently or temporarily taking posession of another body . . . characteristics which remind us unmistakably of the nature of consciousness' is depoliticized when, after all, what is the meaning of haunting if not that the dead are still practicing politics, still fighting their battles, still blessing their constituencies and cursing their enemies?
>
> As for me, I am one of those neurotics, one of those animists, who believes that we can change the world by a mere thought . . . notwithstanding institutional decay, the attack on conditions of possibility for thought by the promulgation of profitable addictions and compulsions in the most sinister of

manipulations . . . such that the posthumous, the afterlife of the institution . . . our so called equal opportunities . . . go rolling off the cliff . . . but we must crawl out of this crash, where we are caught in chiastic rapids, shut out of a stinking calculus . . .

The modest solemn greenery that sanctions us in brochures, pleated up to the sky in marshaled lacework of denial, staring at the desertified plains through our office windows, enlisted to trivia, folded up in our outline, to evade and observe at the same time, our impasse, our morning mindsets and the gelatinous epic of our former plans, withal no simple change of plane, rather a cleaving, tilted sliding, no more the climb along the rough grey gradient of ancestral wish-dreams, an absurd verticality with no upside, the futility of that ascent, of that isolated careering, a devolution away from earthen voluptuousness, time staked for nothing, no, now, festively join becoming planetary: only horizontality, a golden sutra, after nonreaction, atavistic parodies of culture, social neglect, vertical in ascendance, awaken the horizontal dormancy, an involution, an ablution to contingency, to vest in the deferred grace of the impossibly necessary, multiple archipelagos tremble, allow us to un-shoulder that self-preserving guesswork, that artifice of aims, and slowly: to be undone, all awash in a dream of rippling slate seas, the indefinitely rolling waters, acidic with our impasse, overweened by the trumpet of free market fundamentalism blown without cease, the larding of capitalism, its zombie lexicon, collapsing ontology and labor into one, a surrealism of the owning class, while planetary reality itself, is not the property, so to speak, of the market, nor meant to be an object of manipulation for it.

There is not just one invisible hand there are many invisible hands. There are the invisible molecules of carbon dioxide. There are my thoughts, invisible to you, my plans, my imaginings, infinities, totalities, unknown to you. These thoughts, these carbon dioxide molecules, these beings of infinities and totalities are not invisible, as your invisible hand is, with its white glove services, offering degrees like lottery tickets, but now a degree can only refer to a measure of heating, which in turn refers to the measure of state crimes, the daily motion of the sun through the zodiac in another year of political failure . . .

The division of the circle into 360 degrees was known in Babylon and Egypt, while *the degree* certifies knowledge acquired to guarantee the acquisition of other *denominations* standing for properties, abstract coinage the naked aim, the futile achievement of what was never wanted in the first place, at least not in and of itself, for itself alone . . .

§

If she had known how the supervisor felt that day, Jane would not have worried. The supervisor's father had died the week before and she couldn't stop thinking about the nineteen hours in which he was comatose, how his heart kept beating like a little drum even though he was no longer "there" with her. She spoke to him, wept, and sang to him, didn't sleep having learned that hearing is the last sense to go. And now she went through the motions of her job and life in a state of vagueness and desolation, at a remove. When she woke up, she lit a cigarette. The air to her seemed menacing, too thin. She needed to fill it with smoke. She reeked of smoke.

After Jane's talk, the supervisor said, "You're all over the place."

Jane nodded agreement.

The supervisor said, dryly, "I meant that as a criticism."

"If you don't like my words, you can always replace them with other ones."

"You mean I can replace you."

"There is no me to replace," Jane said, "only words."

The supervisor felt tears welling up and could not hold them back. "Are you OK?" Jane asked. The supervisor turned her profile to Jane, a gesture of disdain. She repeated herself about the textbook and left the room. She cancelled her meetings for the rest of the day and drove around in her car, trying not to think.

All the while Jane worked as much as possible on her own project in obedience to the social command. She learned that in Portuguese "social command" was translated as "social commission." She was galvanized by the distinction. *Commission* was more like it. She would accept the social commission, to bring about a world free of command.

In her youth Jane had read Gurdjieff and his student Ouspensky with great thirst and avidity, yet she remembered almost nothing of that oeuvre except for one instruction: *Don't get eaten by the moon*. Perhaps in the same way that computer systems which used to require large buildings came to be compressed within small phones, so entire philosophical systems that take centuries of thought, discussion, reading, contemplation, and writing to develop can, in time, be contained in a small sentence—don't get eaten by the moon.

The violence that her project relied upon, did it signify that she was being "eaten by the moon" of revenge, the machine of hatred? She thought not. She felt she was being eaten by the trees of revelation, not the moon of habit. The few remaining old trees that grew around the neighborhood of the Anarchstery were aware of her, taking her in. Talking to her. And she had begun to speak as them. The trees urged their cause upon her. They urged her to go towards forests, and to destroy, imaginatively, those that would destroy the tree people.

§

One day Jane was reading a letter at an outdoor table at the university cafeteria, situated by a noisy thoroughfare. It was sent by Thomas Mann to Karl Kerenyi in 1934. Mann wrote:

> *My moral-critical conscience is in a state of constant exacerbation, and it is becoming more and more impossible for me to continue pursuing the, it may be, sublime game of novel writing until I have "rendered an accounting" and unburdened my heart of its concern, its perceptions, its pain, as well as of its freight of hatred and contempt.*

She read the passage again and turned over in her mind the possibility of a "sublime game" of art that took the "freight of hatred and contempt" as material. *What is hatred?* she asked herself. *Who are the furies?* Just then she distinctly heard an old woman cursing, bitter and quick, behind her. She felt her heart rock in her chest in fright. She turned just in time to see a child racing by on a skateboard, headphones on, singing.

The child's voice had distorted on the wind and ventriloquized a raging old woman unburdening her heart. And she, Jane, had felt it in her body. *It wasn't intended for me*, she thought, *yet I received it anyway. It didn't happen, yet it happened for me.*

This way that experiences, thoughts, and feelings had of hooking into each other and changing their prepositional positions, crossing as easily as light in, out, above, below, between, and despite bodies, was important for her project. The body was indiscrete, permeable, riven with symptoms, warnings, and signs that came from all directions. The sense doors were utterly vulnerable.

At one and the same time, a person is singing and cursing, young and old. From the perspective of the child, who had never noticed her, whose altered voice had evoked such a reaction in her, she didn't exist. The child was unreal, the old woman real. In some way they were also *one*.

She wrote in her notebook, *worrying so much about our cause, but forgetting that* we *are causes, having effects that we are unaware of; an unconscious telekinetics.*

How can I wed this *species of causality, to* that *effect: indiscernibility, anonymity, unknowability? The way a child could be the carrier of a generational curse, without knowing it, used by ancestors to continue fighting their wars. Spirit the untraceable. Social commissions issuing from the dead.*

That day, Maya decided to surprise Jane on her lunch break between classes. She walked to the university. On her way to the cafeteria, she wandered into the student gallery and watched a video. In the video hundreds of people danced wildly, furiously, thrashing, jumping, quickly gyrating, throwing their bodies around to slow, gentle, ambient electronic music. Then the music and the dance changed. Now the dancers drifted like clouds, eyes closed, barely moving, almost floating, to loud, fast, noise with quick beats and crashing cymbals.

She watched two cycles of the video and then went to the cafeteria where she saw Jane sitting at a corner table at the nearly empty end of a long courtyard, with her back turned. As Maya approached, she heard Jane eating loudly, quickly turning the pages of an enormous book. Maya said, *Mom*. Jane looked up blankly, without recognition, and Maya saw, momentarily, an image of headless forms, of a head cleaving from a body and jeweled red drips, like glittering sap along the side of the neck, in her mother's eyes.

She sat down with a heavy feeling of dread and found herself out of breath.

Jane put her hand on her daughter's back. Maya's throat ached and burned; she asked for water. Jane went to get it.

Maya held very still. If she moved or spoke a single word, she knew she would cry and her cry would turn into a wail, which would bring back breath. But they were in a public place and crying in public was a scandal then, in that culture. In later years, after the beheadings and the regenerations, if one person began to cry in the street, others paused to listen, bear witness, or cry alongside them.

While her mother fetched water, Maya concentrated on the spines of the books on the table, reciting their titles to herself repeatedly until the fear and air hunger melted away and she could breathe again. Over and over, she read the titles silently and as a result, she never forgot them: *Psychic Espionage*, *Anomalous Cognition*, *Reading the Enemy's Mind*, *Remote Viewing: The State of the Art*, *Psychological Warfare: The Rosalind Brodsky Research Programme*.

As Jane filled her water bottle at the water fountain, she did not think about Maya. She thought about her job. Education was a sector rife with turmoil and contradiction. It was a battle over the purpose of existence. Stupidity was no crime, everyone was stupid, some more stupid than others. But how was Jane supposed to reach the patently sad, the increasingly desperate ones, who didn't want to be in school, who didn't want to be anywhere, because there seemed nowhere to be, when she was not supposed to talk, in the ostensible pursuit of truth, about what was true? About how for many students, there was no real home anywhere, no hiding place, no sanctuary? Those who didn't know why they were there—and she understood why they felt that way—what world would there be for them? Where they had been given to believe there was *something* to move towards, they saw *nothing*. Nothingness itself spread everywhere, billowing and featureless, erasing the horizon. The future was much more ghost-like than the past, which was full of life, as if the dead had taken the world away with them, and this was an afterworld. But *there is a future*, the noons knew it, and so did Jane . . .

Jane handed Maya the water. Jane shook her head. Maya braced herself for one of Jane's litanies of disenchantment, which scraped her nerves raw. Maya counted backwards, or made secret resolutions during her mother's perorations, to elide the misery Jane at once described, felt, and transmitted, as if to recruit her daughter to despair.

Maya decided that day that she would simply never talk again. She would be a hermit. She would be as inconspicuous as an ant cutting leaves, or a furrowing earthworm, nude page of the earth, its own body a letter. She had seen how the tongue could leap out of the mouth and attach itself to the ceiling, refusing to come down, like a balloon, how it could run around like a wild dog knocking things over and, just by being itself, destroy the house, tearing up the furniture with its sharp little teeth.

Families are ecosystems that produce specific weather, certain adaptations. Maya's adaptation entailed perfecting the art of not taking positions, of motionlessness and pondering.

She cultivated the stillness of a camouflaged creature who remains in place long after the threat is gone, meditating. She had a feel for the tricks of animals melding into thickets, their hides blending into the foliage. Hides are for hiding and subterfuge. She became an expert at holding still, getting away. During

Jane's jeremiads, Maya's breath would curl up and fail to rise to the lungs and heart, rigidify in her lungs and refuse to sink to the bottom of her torso. She would send a probe into her body. But the more she nosed around, tried to fish for it, the further away her breath swam. Air was all around, yet Maya struggled to get even a sip of it.

On good days Jane formed a canopy overhead, steadfastly filtering the light. This canopy was the real world. Maya would live there someday, when she was old enough, she would leave the sad ground and exist above it all, in the quiet domain of a lambent sky, a hidden bird. Maya would study everything small, as Jane grappled with everything big. Maya looked, for example, into the tiny compound eyes of a moth, each one smaller than a grain of sand, shiny and black, resting on the white slope of a calla lily petal as Jane thought out loud about what kinds of acts brought historical epochs to an end. The moth's eyes seemed to grow bigger as Maya looked. Its torso tapered, pointing, growing smaller at the tail end. Each wing was made of two smaller wings. The upper, larger wing laid on top of the lower wing. The left wing was bigger than the right, more fanned out. It had six silver legs. A tiny joint separated each upper and lower leg at a right angle. They were thin as thread but muscular enough to extend and to fasten onto things. The tips of each lower leg bent ever so subtly, smallest feet, a continuum of the stem of leg. Maya realized the whole flower of the calla lily was a petal, a wrap-around skirt flowing smoothly out of the slender waist of its green shined stem. The moth's lace wings quivered on the porcelain flower, lighted all throughout. Something about the flower reminded her of water. Its clarity and smoothness, a river stone, polished white. Bougainvillea, glistening over walls and fences. White thunderheads with bright silver edges lay mountainous in an otherwise clear sky, swarmed brightly. Maya examined a curious rock, full of holes.

Maya had known it was only a matter of time before Jane quit teaching at the university where she was first a student, then a professor, during their years at the Anarchstery. Jane had held and quit many a job.

When Jane was between jobs the tension drained out of her face and body as if someone had been pounding the dissonant keys of a broken piano and then, suddenly, stopped. As if a machine, a huge, loud machine, had been working and working right in front of you in gale force winds and suddenly the wind died, the machine broke, and everything was still.

Picture a tree growing and rooted. One day, it pulls itself out of the soil. Breaking free of the earth it turns into a cloud. Jane's anger flew away like a bird every time she quit or lost another job. Her relationship with Maya was broken in two by the segmentation of her life, by work. When unemployed, Jane carefully repaired the halves. A delicate sliver of a scar remained, showing the conjuncture, the trace where it would break again.

Between jobs Jane began to think about the public mind as socio-neural architecture. She projected "light sculptures" onto buildings in the middle of the night. She thought of light as thought-like. She used projections to resurface the unconscious of public architecture (state buildings, monuments, libraries, etc.).

To the extent that a signifier, captioned to your incarnate form, could mark you for death, language was an armory of blunt weapons, occluding the fine grain of viscerally subjective experience. "Take the imaginary of what is called *race*," she said to Maya. "Skin is not an image, it is viscera. An envelope of sensations touched softly or roughly, blank, hot, cold, tight, smooth, cut, and so on. And yet the imaginary and the real are conjoined by a kind of political physics in which projections, like entangled particles, move thousands of times faster than the speed of light. They are linked and move in tandem across vast distances."

Maya learned that apartheid states, "epidermal regimes," had made hierarchies according to skintones for hundreds of years. Skins destroyed their own kin in ephochal, genocidal, and planet-destroying terms, which led many to suspect that the earth itself was the site of an alien war game and to give up on knowing reality at all, an epidemic of cynicism. *Appearance is maladaptive,* Maya wondered, *and we will only be free of wars when we no longer appear at all . . .*

Supremacists told on themselves. The hysterical ideology of supremacy had to be taken seriously despite its stupidity because it formed a real distortion field in which violence and exploitation could be irrationalized.

White empire caused the glowing, leaping life of the body to be defined by its pinning to a grid, subtracting movement from the picture to operate the body by the hour on an assembly line, inside a mine, at a school desk, in a field, segmenting flows of time and relation, inhibiting innately unpredictable motions, for when a body is in motion it does not coincide with itself. To force the coincidence, the white hegemon color-coded and scheduled the body, incorporating into its profits fantasies of exception, stereotypes of escape called "salvation" and "luxury."

While some wanted to build energy-intensive systems to draw down carbon and others to spray sulfuric acid droplets into the belly-shaped sky, and still others worked to communize and restrain power companies, Jane intended to prevent the destruction of a livable biosphere homeopathically by means of seven tinctures of death. To justify is to make just, and there was no justification for rule-as-ravage, this was common knowledge. However, Jane was only an imaginary assassin . . .

Can objective problems be solved by imaginary means? Not on the face of it . . . yet, while empirically verified at every scale, the problem was not solely objective, it was also subjective, entrenched in, drenched in mind. Perhaps impossible problems required imaginary means.

In the earliest draft of the *Seven Days of Decreation* generic heads of historical tyrants came detached and fell into a pool and grew into swamp trees. In another series of attempts, she depicted heads rolling along the ground until they fell into holes of flickering black flame and then turned into various kinds of lush and colorful flowers, such as painted birds, gladiolas, and peonies. Then she began to draw then-living heads of current states imploding, spinning, then shattering into fragments that spun in the air and softly settled onto soil as nutriment, like pollen or bursting seeds. No cities would be razed, no toxic clouds would billow up into the sky.

Her approach drew from the fundamentally sculptural, aesthetic, and telegraphic aspect of the proverbial bent spoon, an image the meaning of which everyone can understand—that reality is, in a word, mental.

Jane ruminated on decay as necessity, as spirituality, as aesthetics. From one perspective, the neglect of buildings reflected failure. From another, what went by the name of death in one light went by the name of compost in another. Structures falling, covered in moss, filled with grass, grazed in by passing quadrupeds, taken up by spiders, owls, and snakes showed histories adjacent. Households with photographs on their altars imbued the present with ancestral glances, multiple mindtimes revealed in the faces and gestures of the living and the dead.

Decay, an undoing of knots. Old forms, in dissolution contributed to new ones.

Jane studied images of the right parahippocampal gyrus, the limbic basis for telepathy, in which dreamlike sounds, images, feelings, and thoughts interpenetrate. She saw telepathy as a kind of relational weather. Telepaths studied this seemingly immaterial weather. With attention, telepathic content stabilized and grew more vivid, like a realistic painting getting more detailed over time, or a developing photograph.

Jane developed a method for rhetorically inflecting these nonlocal and yet also metabolic processes, entangling her intentions with those of the bacteria embedded in every organism's plasma membrane, accessible through the *communication of impressions from one mind to another, independently of the recognized channels of sense.*

Jane used a living green pigment she made with chlorophyll appropriating the technique of photosynthesis to convert light energy into chemical energy to radiate effects from afar—as inconspicuously as light—like the sun, 95 million miles away, the great causer.

One might say this is just what language does: it expresses and reproduces structures of feeling. There are those who have even claimed language is a virus. She took the idea literally.

On the one hand, her animations of the decapitations of the seven worst of the necro-politicians, the ones who refused to step down, whose manipulations, violence, and pathological distortion fields forced everyone to think the least interesting and most fearful thoughts, patrolling the borders of what they misunderstood to be *given*, gave her life a kind of organic and radiant momentum. How good it would feel to edit them out of this story, to turn the page, a great turning indeed, a red line through their bloody names, what a "weight lifted" as these pain clowns, these *pressers* (oppressing; depressing) were composted; decomposed; recomposed. They were symbols, living statues to bring down to earth, as a demon / stration.

On the other, there was the barest presence of moral injury, no weightier than a feather, the slightest of moral qualms as evanescent as the word "qualm," a passing shadow of uneasiness in the mind. She held one mouse's life in higher esteem than all the lives of the world leaders who rationed mass death.

For Maya, violence, even in self-defense, could never be

redemptive. She renounced it in all its signs and forms. She wouldn't eat the dead flesh or partake of the eggs or milk of any living body, wouldn't swat a fly.

§

For Maya, the departure from the Anarchstery was sudden and unwelcome. She had never thought of the Anarchestry as temporary, in fact she had assumed it was forever, whatever that was. There was nowhere else she wanted to be: no part of her wanted to leave. What had seemed endless was abruptly over, a broken spell. She neither wanted to attend a different school, nor leave the foggy city and the nines. In this, however, she had no say. Jane was implacable, blunt: *everything changes; must change*. In any case, Jane said, Maya wouldn't have to go to school. Their co-education would continue in the woods. They would learn more living in the forest than they could anywhere else. It was true that Maya would have a larger room in the bungalow, and more time with Jane than before, now that Jane was no longer teaching, and furthermore Maya would no longer have to compete with Enid and the others for her mother's time and attention. She had once longed for that.

Maya skipped the goodbye party and walked around the neighborhood, then got on a bus and rode it for no reason, half pretending to be running away, in a vacuum. Running away to stay? It didn't add up . . .

It wasn't until the morning of their departure, watching Jane and Enid hold each other, that Maya grasped how close they had become. She could see how unhappy they both were. Now her heart ached for her mother. She was alarmed by what was not only the opposite of what she wanted, but possibly a catastrophe, a fall of a kind, impossibly deep.

Enid gave them each a pomegranate and they left, red eyed. Maya looked back to see Enid still as statuary, one hand raised.

§

When she was twenty, after many arguments and debates with Jane about political violence, Maya made a painting to try to render the form of life shaped by the avoidance of violence, to try to explain it to herself. She had long ago decided to be celibate, which was not only a way of avoiding sexual violence but a way of keeping for herself the sovereign responsibility of choice, eliding the state violence of having to register a pregnancy if it happened and the violence of not being able to end a pregnancy that she already knew she didn't want, would never want, were that ever to happen. Her sexual joy vibrated primordially within her, like a secret religion.

The painting resembled a riparian ecosystem. At the center of it, a thin tendril swerved, time and again, away from fear, pressure, threat, pain. This riverine seam bent and curved until it found a place where it could rest and then it became an underground pool. Avoidance of violence finding its level. The shape of a refuge: a hibernator at rest, hidden, solitary, immobile but alive, quietly pulsing with potential, held in abeyance. To refrain, Maya thought, is the key to dignity, and brings subtle, sometimes electrifying delights unavailable to those who never stop doing.

Maya apprenticed to those creatures of winter, latence, and

nascence who existed by almost not existing, who might be mistaken for inanimate, who did not advance, but were instead moved. In this slow time, breathing became delicious, sometimes ecstatic. Why participate in the madness of human history? *All begins in chaos and darkness*, Maya thought, *and then becomes story, which ends again in chaos and darkness, and then begins again, with a new story. One terrible story after another . . .*

For her part, Jane thought of creation as speculative and historical material. "We could be in a simulation," she'd say to Maya, "or we could be part of an indeterminate art project created by an artist in another dimension. Who knows what we are, what existence is? Why not take the social world as potential art? See what you can do with it. Be the creator yourself. The creator! Who destroys for reasons the ancients thought they understood."

"If future history is potential art," Maya countered, "then why use it to recapitulate violence? Considering the historical ubiquity of the 'going back in time to kill Hitler' trope," Maya pointed out, "political revenge fantasies are common. So, where will it end? Fill in the blank, there are thousands of historical candidates for non-birth, people who, had they never been born, the world would have been better. Take your pick," she said, "of dictators, tyrants, colonizers, monarchs, despots, senators, congressmen. Where will the violence ever end?" Maya asked. "How can violence cure violence? Shouldn't we focus on systems? What about 'democratically elected' tyrants?"

Jane was proud of Maya's rhetorical skills. She was not troubled by her daughter's lack of militancy, by her introspective, reclusive personhood. She felt that a world that could not honor contemplatives and solitaries was not worth fighting for. Jane saw that her daughter was one of their number, and it gave her the strength to imagine doing what she would need to do—leaving her. Maya, unlike most, would *use* solitude. She would use her suffering.

"Yes, what about them?" Jane replied. "They make democracy impossible. Elections are like pendulums from which the world hangs by a thread, a parody of mutuality and deliberation."

They were seeding flowers to grow in a large spiral around the bungalow as they talked, flowers that could grow under the forest, in the shade. They had weeded to make space. Jane pointed to the plants they had pulled up, saying, "They are displaced, invasives. The heads of state are also out of place. If they would step down, their heads would not need to roll, and my art would not be needed."

"But if life is imaginary," Maya said, "then they are doing just as you say they should do. They are living their fiction."

"I didn't say life is imaginary. Lacan put it like this: 'Truth has the structure of a fiction.' But there are better and worse fictions to write."

Maya was disturbed when Jane spoke of "the enemy" because it seemed to contradict what she otherwise said about the contingency of categories, and the ignorance of those who saw themselves as separate from each other. She questioned her mother: "Isn't the concept of 'enemy' a reification? Isn't it the enemy's own illusion? *Isn't the idea of an enemy itself the enemy?*"

"Not at all," Jane said. "The enemy is not imaginary, not an alienated part of the self, not a phantom, nor a so-called 'shadow' side. The enemy is extant, objective, specific, nameable. Those heads who obstruct the transition in their corruption, ignorance, cynicism, and delusion, who perpetuate immiseration for self-enrichment, they necessitate their own destruction, and they have names and addresses.

Jane began to render their heads, those leading the drilling, killing, extracting, those who fomented the Never-Ending End of the World.

Some of these heads fervently believed their messiah would not return without apocalypse, and they were right, Jane noted, but only about their own end. The fractal catastrophe of *their* apocalypse would usher forth that collective messiah about whom it has been said *there is another world, and it is in this one.*

§

By the time they had moved to the forest, excepting days when she worked construction and other odd jobs for income, Jane's time was entirely focused on how to use art as a weapon. Rendering the enemy was essential. What and who was it? Certain despots symbolized, by their existence, a curse laid upon the earth. She drew portraits of their absurd and foolish faces. They lay in piles in her workroom in the bungalow or tacked to walls.

To imagine the dissolution, decreation, disintegration, and unbecoming of these men and the murdering, sycophantic apparatuses of impunity erected around them was to feel a great wave of relieved happiness washing over the planet, a great glad tiding, the feeling a body has when it has healed from a deep wound; recovered fully from an accident; resolved finally what had seemed an intractable conflict; healed the broken seam of what had seemed an unbridgeable abyss, an endless impasse.

To symbolize and imagine their vanishing and the concomitant transformation of those who had been snared in their violent thrall, and to see the beauty, love, and intelligence that would arise in their place was more ecstatic than any heretofore known joy. No longer would philosophy be aimed towards death; no longer would it seem better not to have been born, once these torturers were fed to the earth along with their ideological and repressive apparatuses, their militias, courts, corporations, priests, medias, and brokers, everything connected to them that enabled their violence.

There are, Jane had learned in her studies, as many ways to curse and undo curses as can be imagined. In order not to become melancholic, and to deal with their sabotaging violence without oneself being killed, there is the need to symbolically denigrate the enemy from a distance. Sometimes by peeing on their name, other times by setting their image on fire. It is an art form. In ancient Rome they had *defixiones*, curse tablets made of lead. In various times and places, it was only necessary to project the image of your enemy into an object, a figure, and then do harm to that image, for harm to come to your enemy. This act of cursing was aesthetic first, requiring the fashioning of the image of the enemy. Secondly it was personal, social, political. One applied needles and darts to figures, set fire to flags, cultivated venoms against the powerful, buried and drowned the enemy, and of course ritualized beheadings were deployed to bring harm to the signified of the projected image. Knowledge of entanglement went all the way down, and the theater of Einstein's "spooky action at a distance" showed no separation between subject and object, between mind and world. This unity was older than language, older than biota, older than matter—itself derived from consciousness, according to Max Planck.

Words would not suffice, as they drift vaguely, get caught in the weeds of contradiction, go down the drain of circular logics, mired in sloughs of discursive despond.

The stylistic lineage, the house style, the folk genre of the hex, a recourse for the weak, for any community, centers on the paradox of militant rage, highly controlled fury, which can also take the form of a haunting (the Curse of the X) or a possession coming to life to possess its possessor. It's key that the images are projected from a geographically unlocatable source so that it is impossible to know, by normal means, the source of the curse. The normal means, for example, of the forensic procedure, can never catch whoever sets the curse in motion, because there's no physical trace, no evidence (at least not in the limited sense of the physical entailed by conventional detective work). In contemporary militaries, AI, aerial, and drone warfare imitated the Curse of the X: those who died by drone and bomb never saw the faces of their murderers sitting at particleboard desks in windowless rooms.

Before the Great Turning, if there was one thing that could not be denied, it was the imperative to go out and earn all day nearly every day, regardless of how tired or sad you might be. It did not matter if the work was unreasonable, and one could never get caught up. It didn't matter if stacks of papers piled up on your desk. It did not matter if the work was unnecessary or even harmful, if you earned money. Sometimes the price paid for getting paid was explicitly harmful—murdering, deceiving, impoverishing, dumping, poisoning, and imprisoning. Money, the "universal equivalent," the ur metonym of value itself destroyed all other values.

In the early 2030s, during the churning, inventive, and improvisational years of the Great Turning, it was common to find fledgling feminist economists and political geographers cross-training and carousing in the people's canteens, dreaming new equations for ecological democracy. The practice of making transitional objects originated by Napoleon Rosas helped shake people out of their money trance.

One equation circulated widely, drawing from the money-shit metonymy (that money = shit was first discovered by psychoanalysis): profit < shit. In being nutrient dense and lending potency to the soil, excrement was more valuable than profits which, in being symbolic of a form of abstract value predicated on slow (environmental) violence and fast (police) violence, had to be understood not only as less valuable than shit, but—in the emergent syncretic metaphysics—as far worse than valueless.

In exact proportion to their profits, that is also how large a pile of excrement a person contained in their aura, and those formerly known as "the rich" rushed to divest themselves of what had formerly been called "assets" but were now understood to be "asses blooming with shit."

As time went on, the study of categories of excrement, waste, trash, and offal flowered in a new way. The symbolic and metaphorical meaning of these categories would no longer be separated from their biologic, metabolic, chemical constituents. Charity became understood to be the same as "spreading your shit around." To engage in "charity" was to throw shit, like a child or a monkey. It was to try to get rid of some of your shit. The question became, what was this shit called money? What is this excrement called wealth?

The wealthier you are, the more covered in shit. Nobody wanted to be covered in shit, and that was why occasionally they would throw their shit, and this was called philanthropy.

4.

It seemed to her a decision had been made a long time ago, and now Jane would simply embody it: she would bring Maya to Enid, show the films, and then she would go underground. *Underground* was a way to die without dying, to die before they killed you, an exile that kept you free. She would *go to ground* like a fox, or a rabbit.

They had been living for six years in the bungalow in the forest when Jane told Maya, who was now twenty, they were going on a trip to the Anarchstery, to show Jane's film, *Seven Days of Decreation*.

They drove for the first few hours quietly, listening to music and news.

"You know there are always things unfolding that we have no say in," Jane began. "Most things . . . almost everything. We are little aspects, tiny facets of an . . . unendingness . . . which includes its own . . . invisible life-forms, who are always with us." Maya didn't reply. Jane glanced at her; she was asleep.

They passed a group of cows lying down in the shade of an oak tree. Jane pulled over, slowed to a stop.

She searched for the right words. "There has been an . . . exclusivism on the matter of salvation, which contradicts the teaching of unconditional love: that all spiritual traditions are rays of a universal light. It's so important to understand that this universal light is *not* a metaphor. It's the sun itself." Jane stepped out of the car, looked up at the sky and lifted up her arms full of love for the sky.

"We *are* planetary beings, so we are never alone," she went on, "The sun has given us everything. The earth has given us everything. How do we reciprocate?"

Maya opened her eyes with an ache in her neck, instantly forgetting her dream. To her left was her mother outside the car, holding her arms up to the sky, presumably stretching.

§

They would screen Jane's film in the dining hall. Enid helped

Jane set up the practice screening. As it turned out, that was the only time it was ever shown. Enid and Maya, the only audience.

Enid made the following notes about that afternoon.

Jane wanted to do a practice screening of her film and needed help with the setup and projectors. Maya, Jane, and I went to the dining hall where there was going to be a public screening of her animations the following week (which of course never happened) and helped Jane set up.

We arranged a row of seven small tables. On each table was a film projector aimed at the wall and on the table, behind each camera, a thick dossier, documents of the crimes committed by the seven heads of state she had taken as her thesis subjects.

Jane showed us how to run the projectors. Each projector had to be started seven seconds apart. She started the first one and moved to the fourth one. I started the second one and moved to the fifth one. Maya started the third one and moved to the sixth one, by which time Jane had moved to the seventh projector.

The animations showed, one after another, seven recognizable heads of state. My eyes moved from left to right, to see a pattern: each individual film was its own animation, but all together they also made one animation, a kind of flip book.

In each film, one after another, in a cascade, the heads of state came flickering into view. A red woman appeared in the first film emerging from the bottom lefthand side of the frame. A sun appeared above her, casting a subtle, billowing net of light, following the red woman as she glided behind the first head of state.

When the sun first appeared on the screen, a handwritten text briefly flickered across it, "world leader." The red woman plucked the head of the head of state from his body and dropped it.

It rolled slowly down. Intricately, realistically, and microscopically rendered soil appeared at the bottom of the screen just as the head fell into it, planted. The red woman dropped out of the lower right hand of that screen and reappeared on the next one to pluck and drop that head, and so on, through all the films, the sun following along, obligingly shedding light.

A slow downward line was drawn across the neck, a continuous seam between the shoulders as along a bent elbow or thigh, so that rather than a cutting, severing, or wounding, the head simply disappeared down into the neck in a gentle wave. Where the head had been, a sloping, empty bowl-shaped line appeared.

The headless bodies then changed their substances, as the animated woman and sun rose and set behind them, harvesting and planting. The figures, first besuited, then beheaded, began to change form.

In the first animation, the head of a genocidal apartheid state, a mass murderer who refused to step down though the people en masse demanded, fought, and died for it, became mud and cyanobacteria, and we heard creaks and suction.

In the second, an imperialist expanisionist head of state, a lying, thieving, self- and crony-enriching patriarchal opportunist, turned into incandescent light and emanated the sound of a thousand frogs croaking at one helicopter.

In the third, an arms-dealing dictator who let the people starve and sold their farmland to mining corporations became moss and jellyfish. We heard rain, vortexes, and billowing.

The fourth tyrant who neglected and tortured the people and held writers and artists in prisons for decades, became fire, steam, and smoke and we heard cracking glass and whips, engines, and earthmovers.

The fifth, who fomented abuse and murder of people whose religions differed from his, turned to copper, bronze, and iron as the sound of ringing bells, cooking, and the roar of chainsaws and bulldozers filled the air.

The sixth of the sociopathic exploiters-in-chief, poverty-creating and war addicted, who used the people's resources to make missiles and let them starve, was transmuted into papyrus, plastic, and code to the scratching sound of writing, the groan and churn of appliances, the whir of drones, and the click, click, click of vibrating computers.

The seventh head of state, a double-talking, finger-wagging, ideology-dulled, market-worshipping Pollyanna complicitly enabling mass murder, a secretary of ruination and death, dissolved in silence.

Then the red woman, the sun, and the bodies were gone. To the sound of myriad singing birds, whales, and coyotes, all at once complex red flowers appeared on each screen.

Finally blank film leader, which Jane had washed in the ocean, ran through the projector and all we saw and heard was the sea.

§

The correlated vanishing of the real heads of the world leaders who had been depicted in Jane's films, and the sudden bloom of the second set of seven wonders, was something Enid did not try to make sense of. She felt that the boundaries between dreaming, waking, sleeping, praying, and meditating had disappeared completely. Jane also disappeared, along with those demarcations, as if pulling out the threads and pins as she went.

They looked through Jane's things to try to ascertain where she might have gone. It seemed she had taken little to nothing with her. They found two notebooks in Jane's desk about the film project. That her actions would be *unattributable* and *invisible* were, she wrote, not only the condition of possibility for, but, more importantly, the underlying principle of her strike. Under certain circumstances, Jane's notes relayed, light striking an object could excite electrons to generate electromatnetic waves perfectly out of phase, rendering the object invisible. You could make objects disappear by bending light around them. On astronomical scales, the gravitation of black holes warps space to alter the path of light and it was possible to bend light with "metamaterials" which could make objects invisible by guiding light around them like water flowing around a rock so that the rock cannot be seen.

Jane had transcribed a passage from the fulminologist Martin A. Uman on a piece of notepaper and taped it to the wall above her editing table on which her camera, her splicer, her projector, and her notebooks sat:

> *What is important . . . is that the usual stepped leader starts from the cloud without any "knowledge" of what buildings or geography are present below. In fact, it is thought . . . that the stepped leader is "unaware" of objects beneath it until it is some tens of yards from the eventual strike point. When "awareness" occurs, a traveling spark is initiated from the point to be struck and propagates upward to meet the downward moving stepped leader, completing the path to ground.*

Jane had written in red ink beneath the quote, *the method of the unattributable strike is nonlocality.* Enid gathered that the nonexistence of any sender or receiver before that striking exchange—that uncertain liminal and indeterminate state of seeking each other out that can become a strike, or a "revolutionary situation" as it once was called—was central to the enacting of what Jane coined *telekineticature*, a neologism that combines telekinesis and sculpture, and holds the dark lightness of film within it, as a projective force, a vibrating activation of light, redolent of consciousness itself. Jane had come to think of lightning as in some sense imaginative.

Enid read on:

It speculates as it wanders, initiates its stepped leader, wondering: where shall I strike? Sparks from the ground rise to meet it, to direct the questing lightning. The surface, quickened by its presence, engenders the lightning that is engendered by it. The non-knowing of the speculative lightning and blank film leader that is fed into a projector exist in virtuality, as potential, before what will have been. A film begins, lightning strikes. They choose their moment; their moment is now. It doesn't concentrate hard in order to strike from a distance, as we do with telekinesis, moving things with our will, it doesn't strike according to its own will, but rather as a form of meeting, a form of greeting, as an occasion and a gathering of disparate forces. The strike is something that happens between the ground and the sky.

As a student, Jane studied an intra-psychic universe, as logos, inter-animating with subjectivity, agency, causality, and justice. Tacked on the wall next to the Uman passage on stepped leaders was a quotation from one of Jane's teachers, Dr. Karen Barad, responding to Uman:

Injustices need not await some future remedy, because "now" is always already thick with possibilities disruptive of mere presence. Each moment is thickly threaded through all other moments, each a holographic condensation of specific diffraction patterns created by a plethora of virtual wanderings, alternative histories of what is/might yet be/have been. Re-membering, then, is not merely subjective, a fleeting flash of a past event in the inner workings of an individual human brain; rather, it is a constitutive part of the field of spacetimemattering.

Mayakovsky had recommended a "change of plane." To stand back, walk the (eroding, diminishing) distance to the edge of the cliff, edge of the page, edge of time, was the way to divine the true condition of things. This was the quasi-scientific attitude recommended to would-be poets and revolutionaries by Mayakovsky, a Bolshevik who killed himself in 1930, instead of killing Stalin, which would have been, Jane wrote, preferable.

Tyrants and autocrats don't kill themselves often enough. How much better would our lives be if they would simply commit suicide. No hotlines for them! They call the suicide hotline, "I'm thinking of committing suicide." "What's your name, friend?" "Vladimir Putin." "Good idea. Why don't we stay on the line while you go get the pills. I'll sit here with you while you swallow them. Are you sure there are enough?" They save their own skins at all costs, at every cost. Their lives matter more to them than any life, and all life. The definition of dishonor: to put yourself first. The ones who do the most harm hold on the tightest. They have so much harm left to offer, after all. They are never done harming, and they need to live as long as possible, to do as much harm as they can.

Enid found passages that referred specifically to ideas that would find their way into the animations:

As for "world leader," that is the sun, in all its gravity, which leads the planet around and around in circles, causing all earthlings, flora and fauna, to exist episodically, waking and then sleeping in the sun's shadow. This leadership on the part of the gravity of the sun, so serious and so bright, is the purposeless purposiveness of the cosmos. The solar system is the artwork of the sun, while the stepped leader of lightning and the blank leader of film are apprentices of the sun.

In the early days and weeks after Jane disappeared, Maya slept alone in the bungalow and waited for her mother's return. She had a recurring nightmare of the heads of state reappearing in the sky, rotating, orbiting each other, grimacing as they spun, a terrible system of planets, dreadful mockery of the solar system rotating around a vortex that she knew to be Jane.

In her goodbye letter to Maya, a leave-taking that happened without warning, Jane made no mention of when they would see each other again.

She wrote, *I'll be nameless and placeless, as anonymous as a particle.*

Her rhetoric of decapitation began with severing her own ties.

She explained the sacrifice of their relationship in scalar terms. *We wish to make only small sacrifices, but my Maya, we live on a planet, in a cosmos.*

Stars die, planets are pummeled by asteroids, and continents break, explode with fire, and drift. ". . . what is limitless is alone divine and there was neither wall nor road in Eden . . ." (said Margaret Fuller . . .)

§

In one sketch of Jane's animation project on deaccessioning the contemporary patriarch from the decrepit museum of his story, the seven heads implode in slow motion. The fragments become a shower of seeds that fall into soil and nourish the *Amorphophallus titanum*, aptly named the corpse flower, but the stench of this flower was not something she wanted to propagate. In another version the heads become hyacinths, named after Hyacinthus, who was Apollo's boyfriend, killed by Apollo in a sporting accident. From his spilled blood the god conjured the flower in memoriam. She decided against the hyacinth as well, for although the decreations would go unattributed, they should never be mistaken for those associated with an accident, nor taken as homage.

To call the sudden undoing, within a week, of seven heads of state, their *de capitas*—precipitating the end of states, all of them founded on violence, their heads gone—an accident would be like saying that our existence on earth is entirely due to chance, when it is as improbable, as one well-known intentionalist quip had it, as a hurricane blowing through a junkyard over several billion years resulting finally in the construction of a 747. Without intention, so the thought went, the hurricane could blow for all eternity, and a 747 would never come into existence.

As the terrifying and marvelous phenomenon of the transmogrifying and finally missing heads of state rippled through space-time, Maya grieved and struggled to sleep. It took her months to stop fearing the ambient noises the forest and house made at night.

She could not keep track of the dates, the days and hours. Time was jumbled. She thought it was September 27 when it was November 3. She thought it was afternoon, and it was morning. Time did not so much stop as come apart. It wasn't that Jane's absence *obstructed the passage of time she was no longer in* but that she *was* time's passage, and without her time didn't know what to do with itself.

Maya wrote Enid. She wanted to know why they had left the Anarchstery when she was fourteen. Enid wrote a brief reply on unlined notepaper in spidery, frail handwriting.

Dear Maya,

Jane was happy here, and she of course knew you were happy. She felt guilty taking you away. But she felt that staying would prevent her from fulfilling her historical vocation, the "social commission" as she called it.

We can be locked into a version of life merely by repeating it, she said, and sometimes we need to will a change. Practically speaking, to take her work forward, she needed freedom from the obligations of our communal life, which, let's face it, are very time consuming.

We supported Jane, but we wanted you to stay. We argued for it. I told her that she would never need to feel guilt if she lived alone, did her work alone. She could visit you here, and you could visit her there. Remember that. She could have left you with us, she believed in communal childrearing, but she wouldn't even consider it. She wanted to be with you as long as possible.

§

While Maya suffered seemingly unending panic and sleeplessness, desolate with loss, the world was on the mend. Insecure depressions, lonely fears, ecological despairs, suspicion, and money anxiety, all the reasonable responses to conditions created by the genocidal *capitas*, were abating.

Now attention turned to closing the book on the powerholders, their legalized aggressions. Some of those heads who had not been recycled spoke of their childhood dreams, of realizing that as children they had not dreamed of domination and control, of possessing more than others, of violence and alienation. These had never been their dreams, but the haunts of their frightened forebears, which they had inherited. Now they tried to remember: *What were our real dreams?*

Enid, who had worked as a psychoanalyst before co-founding the Anarchstery, found a new use for the old practice of being a janitor of the soul, breathing in smoke emanated from the rim of the subject, and breathing out dreams, listening with the "third ear" to link with and unlock the symptom, refraining from interpreting too soon, attending to that poetry of parapraxis which enables one unconscious to talk to another.

Occasionally she wrote Maya, still living on her own in the forest, about her work. She had been asked to psychoanalyze a few of the surviving heads. One of them was a former CEO of Exxon now working as an eel grass planter at a marine bioremediation site. He was one of those infamous and despised heads whose misdeeds, like Zeus, called down magically appalling storms, yet woke up thinking, *Boy, it's windy today.* The forests where he played golf caught fire, and he wiped his forehead and played on, yoked to the closed loop of his entitlement. He had known that burning fossil fuels led to global warming and lied about it, actively working to misinform the public and delaying action, himself a decoy, a living fake.

Enid wrote to Maya of the prevalence of pathological liars among these corporate executives. *Their inner life is money. They have no true reason. They are all teeth and stomach*, she wrote, *and no heart. They did everything they could to stop change, including putting ungodly amounts of resources into preventing the passage of time—aging—even essaying to live forever. They thought of themselves as the vanguard of the species. They altered everything without ever changing the things that needed to change.*

Confronted with the extent of the harms they caused, some experienced remorse as beaks, claws, suckers, and barbs piercing their interiors. Thorny protruberances seemed to grow inside their gassy stomachs. Their throats grew hoarse with apology. They groaned from mouths dry as canvas hoses, their grey sagging lips tasting of feces, mercury, and blood.

But others were oblivious to the harm they had caused. The CEO of Exxon had lied to his own family for decades. He had led them to believe he was the descendant of a Norwegian king. He claimed to have won awards for archery when he was a child. He said he'd cured himself of cancer through prayer. No one ever challenged him.

When Enid asked him about the effect of his lying at work, he said that it had been part of his skillset, indeed it was a qualification. Everyone in the industry lied. Lying to the public about climate change came naturally. It was just part of the job.

The only time lying had caused him shame, he said, was when his sixteen-year-old daughter asked him to teach her archery.

Unbeknownst to him, she had been given a military-grade bow and arrow for her birthday from her mother, from whom he was divorced. He didn't realize that his daughter liked archery. Why was she interested in it? She told him that she suffered anxiety and depression because of fears related to climate change and wanted to learn ancient survival skills. She had always been proud of the idea that her father knew archery.

He told her that climate change was a hoax, and furthermore he didn't remember how to do archery. She looked down, and he could tell she knew he was lying. He told Enid that in that moment he had felt a sharp pain in the back of his neck, like a guillotine.

Enid suspected he would lie to her too, and that perhaps everything he had told her so far about his lies were also lies. She noticed herself becoming withdrawn during their conversations, incapable of questioning or challenging him. It was as if she was being forced to accept his lies in silence. The fact that Enid felt that she couldn't say anything in the face of his dissimulations, that she was compelled to withdraw into resigned silence, showed, she wrote to Maya, what was at the root of political impasse.

Another analysand of Enid's, a congressman who had repeatedly blocked climate action to protect his investments in coal, behaved like a convert, veering into hyperbole. As he described his new life remediating mountaintop mines, his voice was loud, compulsive, jumpy, and incessant. Enid felt depleted by him. He used the terms "amazing" and "profound" over and over. Yet nothing was amazing or profound. Instead, there was just exhaustion, as if he was blowing himself and his experience up, to mine it for energy. Enid thought he was avoiding the torment he would feel when he faced the devastation he had caused, warring on mountains.

One day, as he was going on, Enid closed her eyes and went to sleep. She woke up after a while. He was looking at her, in humiliated silence. "You fell asleep while I was talking." She smiled, refreshed, and said, serenely, "You're a blowhard." He suddenly felt as if the top of his head was the bottom of a long, flat scoop, or plate, that curved slightly up at the sides, the top of the head hollowed out. He felt waves gently rolling from one side of his cranium to another, a soft, rolling fluid pulsing in the head. He began to shake and cry. Now he wept with desolation, despair, grief, and regret. He described therapy as an interrogation and seemed to expect retribution for the role he had played. But Enid kept asking him to think about the effects of his actions: What about the toxic noise he had made in the world, the ruinous explosions?

Once Enid asked him how it was that he and his like had not seen the extinctions they were causing, endlessly expanding the fossil economy, constructing power plants, grids, mines, wires, ensnaring propertyless workers in the game of surplus-value extraction, like so many units of expansion, driving farmers from their land, congregations of hunger, displacement, and carbon intensification arising concomitantly all in the name of driving "investment." "How did you miss it?" she asked. "Did you believe your own lies about so-called 'development'?" He said, "I did believe it; I accepted that people would have to be sacrificed. I thought, it's all over already, it's too late. It wasn't me, right? It's the system. That's what you people always say:

we're interchangeable parts in the system. I'm not responsible, am I, if 'it's the system,' and anyway what could I do? I couldn't stop the inevitable."

Enid wrote:

Some of them talk of a sick, poisoned feeling they have always had. They talk of feeling nothing for years on end but clammy fear, licking them under their skin, and of the sadness they felt about their children's despair, their inability to focus or sleep without drugs.

Enid played Shostakovich's tenth symphony for the former Exxon executive, a favorite of his. They talked of how the composer had made beauty out of fear in a state of creative terror. "Your propaganda has caused exponentially more death than Stalin did," she commented. He began to shake uncontrollably.

5.

Jane had cast herself into the gyres of transformation, the key to which was not redistribution of wealth and the abolition of work, but the reverse: the redistribution of work and the abolition of wealth. Pollution-related diseases proliferated from all directions, from mining, industrial chemicals, commercial agriculture, nonferrous metal production, electronic waste recycling, air pollution, foul water, the poisons of domination and exclusion, and the abandonment of the precautionary principle in favor of maximizing exploitation.

To work together was to contend with waste, not leaving it to someone somewhere else to die of, but claiming it, in equality.

To be was to be beholden to this toxically industrious inheritance.

Those long laid low by working and living proximal to toxins were cared for and healed in detoxification cooperatives.

The only property one could "own" any longer was one's "own" toxicity and waste, yet some had been forced to "own" toxicity their whole lives—they died of where they lived.

Not a redistribution of wealth, but the abolition of wealth and redistribution of work centered, in the beginning, on pollution where the responsible parties were either unknown, bankrupt, or obsolete state agencies, "legacy" contamination.

No one had been held liable for the contamination in such cases, half of which were from the mining industry. Many of these sites had gone unremediated up until the time of the composting of the heads, when councils harmonized localities and municipal cooperatives proliferated.

Once the categories "worker" and "boss" were dismantled, labor disalienated, companies cooperativized, people began to practice repair in their own communities themselves, drawing on traditional and emergent techniques, integrating local and technical knowledge. It was fun and difficult to heal the land, to learn how.

Projects all over the world involved remediation of ordinary contaminations arrayed molecularly everywhere, a hazy pointillism of dichlorodiphenyltrichloroethane, polychlorinated biphenyls, hydrocarbons, mercury, tannery waste, aluminum, cyanide, fluoride, used lead–acid battery recycling, uranium, nickel, and radionuclides consisting of cesium, strontium, plutonium. The model of excavation and safe storage where contaminated soil was physically removed and stored somewhere off-site had not healed the soil. The old mitigatory attitude towards excavation and storage for hazardous waste only made industrial contamination seem something fateful, inevitable. Sickening by poison was treated as the inescapable underside of being a person.

Throughout the Great Turning, work was understood as something, like death and symbiosis, that all beings do together. The first thing children learned was that nothing living is un-symbiotic. Every child knew the cow can't digest grass or the termite lignin without their bacterial communities to do it for them.

Wave after wave, fold after fold, of symbionts plying for each other's trade, over millennia the original barter system would heal contamination. The people awakened, like the Seven Sleepers of Ephesus, to a changed world, to subtractions of old alienations that made room for new intimacies.

Damaging parasitics were trained upon each other to self-devour. For example, surveillant police states were turned in on themselves through mirror magics: cameras filmed other cameras filming other cameras filming other cameras, ad nauseum, swallowed into infinite nothingness, so that all the police saw were other police seeing other police, in an infinite police fractal that had no outside, until policing sloughed away, like so much dead skin, along with nation-states.

Currency's purpose drained away as gifting economies reemerged. Assemblies all over the world discussed the ethics and aesthetics of indebtedness, ways to disalienate debt, drawing richly from poor theory. As these discussions went on, people began spontaneously to create transitional objects after Napoleon's model, which the children of the Anarchstery popularized as they grew up. They came to be called *subjunctives*. Napoleon described them as counterfactual projections, conveyances for the circulation of providential futurity.

From the beginning they were exquisite artworks made almost entirely from recycled materials. Subjunctives expressed the relationship between giver and receiver, for instance in one famous early example, a plumber carved from stone a one-legged figure with a head where their foot would be, and a tall wing where their head would be, to describe the somatic freedom they felt as ephemeral living artworks called "Becoming Chimera" conjured into being through the medium of the body by means of a three-hour massage which made them feel they could see, smell, hear, and taste the earth through their feet, made their head feel light and spacious, sent their mind into flight, and sent pleasurable currents coursing through their entire body. The bodyworker accepted the sculpture in trade.

Other celebrated examples of early subjunctives depicted intersubjectivity and symbiosis in myriad ways. The emptiness of giver and receiver was a theme. These tended to be full of holes (conceptual and material) and became a recognizable genre.

The subjunctives ranged from contemplative ritual objects to monuments. The global instantiation of Indispensable Universal Elemental Providence included enough nourishing food, clean water, protective and restorative shelter, meaningful work, earthly stewardship, spiritual care, egalitarian education, downtime, and holistic healthcare for all to thrive. Because everyone traded regularly, everyone, without exception, made art and made it often, so a world that had once been full of waste was now full of art.

§

When the heads disappeared, a carnival overtook the world for some time. In the first months of the great transformation, an antic, festive, and joyous mood prevailed. Societies were reconfiguring with dizzying constancy. While some were "dizzy with excitement" and "dizzy with joy" some who had for so long been numb with fatigue were at first nauseated, stricken with a kind of "morning sickness" as talkative, space-traveling bipeds linguistically and culturally distinct, comprised of pluralities and clamoring for "the right to opacity for everyone" collectively underwent the death of violent hierarchies. Some experienced the Great Turning in overwhelmingly physically pleasurable ways as if sex had appeared in the world for the first time, as if the universe turned out to be sex itself.

The fascists and bullies who had been supported and protected by the high officials that worked under the heads of state became disorganized and pensive. Work stoppages, hunger strikes, and rebellions led quickly to the demise of corporations and their conversion to cooperatives.

De-enactments replaced re-enactments, as people wriggled out of ill-fitting garments of history, the suffocating hand-me-downs of patriarchy's wars. A certain contingent of the awe-struck came together for a week every year to ritualize the recycling of the heads, hoping by means of ceremonial pageantry they could assimilate the break from the old story and build connective tissue into the future, the new epoch of repair. *From despair to repair we reweave the biosphere*, they sang.

In particular, the end of the never-ending end and the beginnings of beginnings had stunned those systems thinkers who thought that getting rid of a few corrupt leaders would never make enough of a difference because, as they used to argue, there were an infinity of them waiting in the wings. "It's the system," they would say. "We can't be distracted by the individual, sociopathic despots. We must fundamentally end the system. The parts of capitalism's machines are interchangeable. It's the machine, not the parts, we need to destroy."

And yet, de-creating the right number of despots, in the right order, at the right time, at the right hour, all in a row, knocking them down like bowling pins, an occult strike, to nourish existence in all its forms, flowering for its own sake, was a difference that made a difference such that all the organizations and projects *made to make a difference*, to dream forward the liberatory world, the good road, stepped out of the wings of political theater, out of the emergency rooms of political crisis, out of the waiting rooms of political history, out of the understory of political wilderness.

The focus on healing and change pervaded everything; new fields of experience opened, reconfiguring human existence, while Maya felt increasingly closed off, undergoing a contraction that seemed to have no end, a falling that seemed to have no bottom.

Maya's loneliness, pain, and isolation were unremitting at the outset. For some time, she could find no relief from her abyssal distress. She was not merely on the outside looking in, she was nowhere at all. She reproached herself for her incapacity to feel joy, to be changed. Her shock kept her awake. As a result of not sleeping for days on end, there was no alternation, no pattern, as if her capacity for experience had simply ceased. She often wondered if she was dying or perhaps already dead.

The relieved disorientation of those who danced with happiness and awe merged with Maya's stunned agony as she gradually realized that Jane was not coming home. All emotion felt like one indistinguishable, inextinguishable fire in her body, and she simply burned. Or numbness crept through her, and she went rubber limbed, immobile. To grieve was to ail. She was a hot lung, radiated with condensed sorrow. Then a switch, and here came a fluted, cold, dried-up throat.

She traveled around looking for Jane, going here and there from project to project, ostensibly joining in with everyone else to rebuild and remediate society, to feel and find her way with others into the new rhythms of cooperative autonomy.

When this time of grief, of burning and icy, blank lightness ended, after looking for Jane she returned to earth.

On her twenty-third birthday, she spent the day alone. Jane, the instrument of her life, of her happiness and sadness, was now sense-memory. She let her go.

Giving Jane up was like putting on an old familiar coat, handed down generation after generation, heavily patched, weighted, and protective, dusty, and prickled, difficult to bear, yet necessary for reasons she did not comprehend. She lived in the bungalow feeling a loneliness that seemed to pervade the entire universe, looking inside herself for something unnameable. A cure?

The trees, insects, rabbits, squirrels, birds, snakes, and lizards who lived there had nothing to do with what had happened to her. Their activity was a lesson in ongoingness. In being equal to life.

One day she took a spider in hand that had been stuck indoors for days so that she could bring it outside. It held still, let her carry it. Without her realizing it, this was the tiny, incremental-eyed beginning of the end of her loneliness.

She sat on the ground and drew the spider as it waited for an impulse. Then she made a drawing of the round line of water, poised in glass.

§

Mostly they used to be broke. Maya and Jane had languished on what money they could, until finally, money went down the drain, and then after Jane left Maya lived, as everyone did, on the startlingly adequate provisions of the Great Turning. She did her share of labor when called, pitched in with childcare, treeplanting, remediating light pollution to support migrating birds and near-shore invertebrates, worked stints at the listening posts taking notes on what was needed, to bring to the great assemblies. The projects were variously coordinated and orchestrated, and everyone participated in their own way. Four to thirty hours a week for three or four months a year sufficed. The rest of your time was self-determined.

Sometimes she stayed at the Anarchstery and did her service there, helping with the many projects the no-ones spearheaded. This allowed her to see Enid and Cass.

But Maya spent years, decades, largely in solitude, in the clandestinity of private life.

Silence after silence. The silence held numberless feelings, weather, languages, questions, memories, daydreams, reveries, powers, and sensations, arising and passing away as she sat, thoughts like bubbles popping, like so many animals of every size and shape in their season.

Some years she felt herself floating up to the sky on a golden pyramid and everything shimmered for months on end. Other years she traveled without moving in the canopy or along the humming ground, sensing every root, every bird, every ant.

She developed the capacity to feel beyond the strata of atmospheres, where gravity's field of play jumped scales. There she encountered planet-organisms akin to earth.

Eventually, in her quiet sitting, she traveled through multidimensional realities far beyond the "deep time" of geological earth. So much time folded into so many folds.

When she was in her early sixties, on a Tuesday, in her tenth hour of meditation, one of these lineations called to her, named Aster. A pulse went back and forth between herself on earth and this not-quite-endlessly-distant but nearly indiscernibile and subtle point, where Aster listened.

Maya prayed for Jane to be alive and safe, and to see her again before the end. To pray for this was to solve the past, the present, and the future all at once. She conceived her own afterlife as held in the safe hands of Aster, with whom she would merge in the end. She remembered Aster from a long ago dream as the being she had run towards, for safekeeping, while her mother did what she had to do, delaying Maya's birth with peacock flower tea, an abortifacient.

Although many had said that death was valueless (that "it has not required us to keep a day free") Maya had come to see that it was not a question of value or nonvalue, of good or bad, but rather, as Mayan texts described, it is death that enables star people to establish bonds with planetary travelers—the dead.

Maya had learned from reading Jane's notebooks that she believed creation was not the work of a single creator, but the result of an ill-thought-out set of intentions, a game someone began to play and then abandoned, as if someone were to plant experimental seeds in experimental soil and then go on a trip, forgetting the whole thing, never to return. The creatures who were the content of the experiment now had to "run the lab" themselves. Politics was the question of whether to allow certain products of the experiment who were rancid with existential discontentment to cause the whole thing to self-destruct, or to allow other products of the experiment, in love with creation, to realize its potential as an artwork.

In the end, Jane chose the "Lucifer" cultivar of the crocosmia for her metaphor, a flower that was the definition of red. In the film, the heads would have a place in the ecosystem, because Jane imagined that the damage they inflicted was due to existing in the wrong role. In the animated film, they were recomposed into a fungus beneficial to the so called "Lucifer" crocosmia. They, being evil, would nourish these "flowers of evil," and this would be a redemptive role for them.

By means of *telekineticature*, Jane projected the animations directly into the heads of state. During the one and only screening of the films, with Maya and Enid as the only audience, the respective heads of state dreamed their own detachment.

There was no explanation for the sudden bloom of a fungus beneficial to crocosmia "Lucifer" so that everywhere in the vicinity of where the heads had lived, these flowers grew taller and bigger than they ever had until they were as tall as trees. They became a shocking phenomenon, growing in some cases as tall as skyscrapers such that their fan of red blossoms provided shade, filtering the light down on those below, pointing in wonder under the glinting plants, looking so much like green knives dripping blood.

Public assemblies, conducted in myriad idioms, vernaculars, and idiolects, focused for some time on analyzing and disentangling causes and effects. An entrenched discursive reversal, a compulsory principle of delusion, a deadly formalism, an infected tunnel: racism, classism, sexism, and genderism had been misconstrued as causes of their own occurrence! While in fact they were effects, the (ir)rationales of exploitation, extending the taxonomic practices of ethology, which disguised the invention of "lower orders" among humankind as a given, as a *cause*.

Gender is the extent we go to be loved, one writer suggested. Gender unfolded in the first-person. In truce, gender faded, an affectionate old mural. What had been endlessly problematized as if it was a cause, came to be understood as an effect, and what had been misunderstood to be an effect, was revealed as a cause.

Being forced to take stupidity seriously caused madness, mass neurosis, scattered and fragmented psyches, and deadly hatreds. The figure of the dangerous white clown was ubiquitous. Satire nearly went extinct as figures of absurdist critique turned geopolitics into a nightmarish allegory of itself.

The entertainment industrial complex had rehearsed the apocalypse so many times, without pause. Melancholic class formations which caused mass depression and had been instituted through nomenclatures of exploitation and commodification were undone. This de-creation caused mass vertigo . . . a kind of rainfall in the mind. And then spring. Those modes of production which had divided humankind into either labor or capital, master or slave, servant or owner—histories rendered in stories such as *Germinal*, *Metropolis*, *The Grapes of Wrath*, *The Gift of a Cow*, *Life in the Iron Mills*, *Blood on the Forge*, *Things Fall Apart*, *Red Star*, *Beloved*, *The Dispossessed* and so many others—would no longer be the subject "realism" but would be undone in reality. The relentless "patriarchal realism" of the entertainment industrial complex with its endless boring apocalypses died away. Only by virtue of being strange, uncanny, terrifying, unattributed, and unclaimed could *telekineticature*, a social sur / realism, work.

"Someone" would have reignited all the old wars, Maya knew. The secret was to keep the secret: Jane's clandestinity.

That *no one* was behind it was what allowed everything to change. It was deterrence of a new kind. A return to primordial humility, hidden causalities, to open the hand. This hidden *no one* was not the same as the *no one* of Maya, who, by hiding away, hid nothing, left things untouched.

Afraid of being composted in the same mysterious manner, those who had tried to elide their own deaths by making others die instead, who had made a metaphysics of inequality, stuttered and fell, leaving only a residue, a faint, gassy mire.

6.

Decades later, long after the beheadings, although Maya still had not seen or heard from Jane, she sensed that her mother was alive. She felt her heartbeat still pulsing somewhere on the surface of the earth. Jane had gone underground, but was not yet *underground*, not yet rejoined in the upsidedown sky of root systems, the lively heaven below. Maya would have felt the earth tip, if Jane had gone down to the underworld.

Maya began to write her own philosophy as her mother had before her. She drew and conjectured about underworlds.

Root systems give all their meaning to the word, the concept, weight. Earth is gravity itself, is grave, so why hate growing down, or death? Mountains are a risen weight, seas bowls of weight-bearing weight. Tsunamis break new lines between the land and sea. Mountains break apart and the land slips down. A mountain buries itself. When the land is logged and stripped, mono-cropped, root systems that once held the soil in a strong weave are destroyed, the soil grows flighty, rootless, and it runs away.

What's the nature of that which refuses to decay, fall apart, to go down, be done with? Compare a microwave on its side by a swamp, or a suitcase in a river, with the bones of a flying squirrel. The tyrannical cells of the sore loser who refuses to concede with the humor of the good sport who knows the game is change. Compare the infamous "black mayonnaise" of toxic sludge that killed so much marine life, to the ink of squid.

Deterioration is also one of the muses, the unmentionable ones.

Instead of inspiring, the muses of decay expire.

Occasionally people would come by and check on her. She gave them clothes and books. They left her with grains, legumes, fruits, vegetables, tea, coffee, and chocolates.

Maya didn't think of herself as solitary, but that was the way she was seen.

There was a poignance to her obvious vulnerability. Her visitors could see that the house was compromised, giving way. They didn't force the issue. It was up to her to bring up her problems in the new dispensation, where the autonomy of elders and children was respected and the old condescensions dropped. Maya didn't care to collectivize the problem of the house sliding, nor move. Nor did the house wish to move, though it had come loose, lifted off the horizon. They would both be moved. The problem . . . it was her companion. Perhaps a holdover of the old occultation. What it meant to be both monkey and monk, a long-lived child.

When the house falls, it will have fallen, Maya thought. Until then everything hovered indecisively, expectantly, ready to leave at any moment, to return to another life, or to escape this one.

Then she would forget all about the sliding house, hum a tune that came out of the thin air, seemed to be given to her by the clouds.

Sometimes sitting at the bottom of the ravine that threatened the house Maya felt a change of plane stealing over her spirit, for example when she suddenly noticed the dogwoods had bloomed again. But hadn't they already come and gone? What year was it?

As a small child, the apartment building where Maya lived with Jane was near a weedy lot. She watched the swallowtails in the mallow flowers that grew there, along walls covered in faded graffiti and murals.

Maya remembered the improbable nasturtiums and clovers as well as the children she sometimes played with, some of whom went home to families who didn't hesitate to beat and denigrate them. It was thought one had a right to harm one's children.

After the ending of the end and the beginning of the beginning, every newborn was woven a vestment with a pocket on which was written the ethos that children would be raised free of violence, exploitation, intrusion, and insult. Their lives would not be seen as rehearsals for life.

Like the blooming of those flowers that open as soon as they are set in water, certain things that seem unimaginable and impossible happened instantaneously. No longer would child rearing be a cause of isolation, poverty, exhaustion, desperation, and the passing down of family curses. Over the months and years, those who had been *building the new world in the shell of the old* helped a learning society come to the fore.

§

In the old times, one charted the days as a course of panic and rushed quickly about getting something over with, but the sudden cessation of fossil fuel traffic due to oil supply chain breakdown brought a profound quiet. A hush fell across waterways and airways and highways and quickened the spin of the planet through space so that the basic laws of physics underwent a temporary shift, the result of which was that each time one ventured across the threshold and walked two or four or seven steps into the world's fresh changes, one's spirits lifted free from their old bindings, and in this way all floated and hovered.

Creeks came out from under sidewalks, seedlings sprouted along the liberated banks, bears splashed in swimming pools, coyotes slept in abandoned motel beds, bears denned in tool sheds, wildlife migration corridors proliferated as multilane freeways fell into disuse and were quickly overtaken with grasses and seedlings of trees and wildflowers.

The earliest global, collective, post-collapse project, eventually known as the micro-cosmosis, was the conversion of built environments so that anyone could live, eat, get medical care, healing, rest, work, make art, meditate, and study wherever they were. Once the public's sanity was restored by the meeting of basic needs, ecological praxis and remediation called to them, wherever they were, as there was no place where it was not needed. Meeting basic needs was social sculpture.

Initially the micro-cosmoses were a temporary arrangement, a way to universalize housing and food relations ("food relations" because food is a metabolic partner not a passive substrate). But they proved both convivial and effective, and remained, and grew. Their architectures were modeled on honeycombs with shared walls that bulged, curved, and stacked. People intuitively began to situate shared dwellings on curves and spirals again.

When it came time to redefine work, it turned out to mean you did a lot of things. You learned a lot of what used to be called "skills" (as if the singing, nesting, and flying of birds are skills), found your animal know-how. Some forms could be (and were) adopted and adapted. For example, the simple provisioning of lists of activities and work details, trainings, and groupings, for which people of all ages could sign up, to work, facilitate, and learn.

It was felt that the many demanding, complex tasks, and real, necessary projects that needed doing were school enough. It made no sense to wait for children and young people, with all their clarity, inventiveness, and vision to "finish school" before joining in with the work.

The nonlinear, seemingly "unproductive" aspects of learning were respected: sleeping, daydreaming, disinterest, skeptical resistance, lying on the floor, throwing a tantrum, wandering off, getting lost, arriving late, and making mistakes.

Before, there were those who "owned" private property according to the old system, who believed in it then and still did.

There were those who had private property according to the old system, who had never believed in it.

Those who held no property, but nevertheless believed in it, feared losing what they never had.

Those who held no property and never believed in it were ready for change.

Commonly, human people belonged to terra in the same way that fish belonged to water and birds belonged to sky. There was no reason to steal what was already yours, just as a fish didn't steal the water it swam in, and birds didn't steal the sky, and death was no exile from life.

People of every age, even great-grandmothers, used to make use of sidewalks as beds under streetlights. The itinerary of a wanderer, once called "transient," without access to commons and therefore without access to sleep, was endurance itself. For lack of a sloping wall or sheltering roof, shouting was used to create a force-field of protection, a voice churning up from the well of abandonment, exile, displacement, rejection, exhaustion beyond measure, and above all war.

Picketers and marchers walked in great circles to try to draw a line against the expropriating mouth through which their labor threatened to be sucked into the black hole of a nothingness, until the only thing heard throughout the universe was the sound of slurping.

What was once derogatorily called "social services" was built upon along with all that had once been categorized as "public" from schools, parks, and libraries to "assistance" and housing. Self-governed autonomous zones around the planet had seen the way forward, planting seeds of sacred public joy and participation.

If humans could, and did, de-create a liveable planet by rooting action in imaginary concepts, such as the fiction of private property or dominion or supremacy, then perhaps humans could recreate a liveable planet by imaginative means. This was Jane's wager, though for Maya it had always been impossible to separate imaginary and actual violence. Her mother had never seen or played the violent video games that poisoned the psyches of Maya's generation, used for military recruitment. Inhabiting the virtual shooter persona made killing a game so that life itself became unreal. For Maya, if imaginary violence became real (which is why soldiers train, and why predators play fight) so might imaginary nonviolence. Nonviolence made life real again.

Why dream a bad world?

§

Maya joined projects intermittently. The work she did entailed biodiversifying monocropped plantation forests, planting mutually beneficial trees and understory, and healing depleted agricultural fields with a range of techniques from planting symbiotic families of cultivars and remediation with biochar.

Maya found she liked work, if not the conversation. The people she worked with learned to respect her taciturnity and let her be. There was a particular feeling that would come over her, that she had been among people for too long, and it was time to go.

Technically she no longer owned the bungalow. At times people passed through, lived with her briefly, or camped nearby for a day or a week or a month, used her kitchen and then moved on. Sometimes she was there with them, sometimes not.

Maya would go to the old cemetery and sit as still as a statue under an enormous rhododendron. A tremendous inertia would overtake her body. By the shrines of ancient personages, she felt herself becoming enshrined. She moved so slowly that it took all morning to travel from wherever she had slept—the couch, the floor next to the bed—to the coffee pot, and as much time again to find the front door, to open it, and to behold the changed world into which Jane had vanished.

Perhaps she would fall asleep and stop breathing right there, in the presence of the yellow sun, the blue sky, the brown earth, and the red flowers. Her own house would fall on her, she'd be entombed with the remnants, the miscellany of life and the debris of history like those ancestors who packed furniture, clothes, honey, jewelry, weaponry, spices, art, and keepsakes for their passage to the afterlife, all that equipment abandoned, like the body to the spirits. The spirit jumps right out of form.

The house could fall and Maya with it, just another object sacked, thrown off course, her flesh, bones, nerves, cells, so much bric-a-brac. *At that point*, Maya thought, *we, me and all these household objects would look around and find our tentative attitude, our disbelief, our way of floating noncommittally one inch in the air, finally justified.*

Is there anything that is not unsettled, not uncertain, not mismatched, out of place? There was no longer any reason to try to put things in order.

§

Maya was increasingly forgetful which was not a problem, but she didn't want to forget Jane. She decided to write down what she remembered about her mother's philosophy, before she forgot that too.

Jane was of the intentionalist school of art who, in contrast to the creationists, believed the universe was not a design or a creation, but an intention, governed not by laws or rules, but by unpredictable interactions. It was too flawed to call it unified. Rather, existence, creation, was an idea—a young and incomplete intention, perhaps even a mind having a thought.

Intentions are uncertain, which is why the theologians used to speak about our unfinished-ness, and why every human being feels that they are receivers of some task. The task is to carry forward the intention, to test it, to see what could come of it through enaction. As an artist, Jane knew that, for a given piece, to get the feel that nothing is missing required severances—cuts.

We can't be sure that what we start won't take on a life of its own, won't be taken up and completed in ways we never imagined by those whose own intentions have nothing to do with ours; for example, look what happened to the old revolutions, look what the heads of state did to the color red. Red, which darkens and brightens . . .

A creationist might say, well then, who intended the universe? To which the intentionalist might reply, the unintended . . . who is not a subject.

§

When she was seventy-two, Maya received an antique postcard. It depicted the unmistakable shaft of a mine, a cross between a sentry tower and a treehouse, with a mirrored strip of watery foreground. The handwriting, though faint, was recognizably Jane's cursive with its wide loops and large letters. In the postcard Jane briefly explained that she had been living at a former plutonium plant, remediating the site.

Many who worked there were terminally ill, and she was one of them. She had been called to this taxing, toxic work of remediation and had done it for fifty years. She had not wanted Maya to be exposed to it, did not want her to get sick.

The plant where Jane had moved was used as a permanent disposal site for processing thousands of tons of exhausted fuel elements, with a half-life of 300,000 years. Nuclear waste had been imported to this site from places all around the world. The disposal of the tons of waste had, formerly, garnered the region the largest quantity of superfund site aid to date, which went towards enriching those involved and even citizens of the local town, while the waste continued to leak and seep into rivers and root systems. After the Great Turning the most toxic remediation sites such as this one were made into sanctuaries with dedicated attendants, on the model of monastics, who would guard and heal the site. Like the first nuclear weapon, the universe had been determined to be a dodecahedron by the wavelength of microwave radiation's harmonics which, like any musical note, reflect the shape of the object in which it is generated.

The knowledge that energy into shape equals function was used to create shape-note songs that, sometimes very slowly, sometimes instantaneously, rendered harmless the molecular composition of toxics. With others, Jane learned to detoxify and contain the toxic waste, and passed down the knowledge of how to do it. There was a return address. The next day Maya ate breakfast and packed a bag. The sun had barely risen. She walked slowly for a half-day to the nearest train station and boarded the train.

For sixteen hours she looked out the window of the train with an empty mind at an empty sky. Whatever her life had been between the moment of Jane's vanishing and this one, of her reappearance, was a blank frame of film. A book of pages so faded, it may never have been written, including those hundreds of pages inscribed with fantasies and dreams of reunion, which had consumed Maya for so many years.

The past had folded in on itself and she was a daughter again, returning to her mother, to be together at the end.

It was nothing like her fantasies: It was simply real. Her mother was alive but dying. The world had changed in all ways, while change had remained itself. It has been said that all beings partake of a figment, an element of divinity. What else was this element, but change?

Halfway to her destination, she spent a night sleeping in a cot under a large canvas shelter in a field, open to all comers. The field was strewn here and there with giant old "leave" trees. Over time their canopies spread out, these wolf trees, with long, wide, curved, and bent branches the size of small trees themselves. They were flocked with crows, stuffed with acorns, ornamented by nests, each tree a city of animals.

The night was hot, the sky clear, stars thickly strewn across the ceiling of the night like spilled beads. She slept. When she woke up, she felt mineralized, like a statue who has miraculously opened its eyes, astonished to be alive. The air was balmy, though clouds roiled and hovered. Flashes of light cracked along the distant horizon. Her eyes were sore at first, but that dissipated as she studied the land.

She walked in quickly rising heat at a slow pace, pausing for breath and water, to catch the second train, which took her to the former superfund site where her mother lived. When she arrived, two people awaited her. They took her to the community center where Jane lived. Jane had packed one small bag with a broken zipper. Maya recognized it, though it was blackened with stains and age. They slept one night there and departed the next morning.

Jane marveled at the coolness and the rain, having lived in a dry, hot desert for so long. She smiled at everything, amazed that, at least inside, the house was unchanged. Even her project notes, faded to whiteness, were still pinned to the wall of her workroom. She noticed the tilting of the house, the encroachment of the ravine, but did not remark on it.

For Maya feelings as old as her life, and maybe older, surfaced in waves.

Jane didn't talk much. Most of the time, she slept. She spoke of a metallic taste in her mouth that never went away, the poison she had absorbed, made herself the recipient of, as an agent of detoxification. Not seeking to rid herself of it, to cast it elsewhere, but to take it in, to take it upon herself, the stigmata of industrialization. Jane spoke of many cases where cleanup of heavy metal and pesticide contamination had failed for decades because community members who knew the sources of the pollution were never contacted by companies or governments.

Maya turned on several small solar lamps which rotated, looking around and sending warmth. She got out blankets and shawls, colorful and warm.

One morning over breakfast, sitting at the round table Jane had fashioned lifetimes ago out of an old shipyard cable spool, Maya spoke about the animations Jane had made that had tipped the whole world into the light of justice and repair. Unsure if Jane would be up for discussing it but knowing that this might be her last chance to do it, she asked Jane what it was like to be the catalyst, the hands at the wheel of the Great Turning.

Jane raised her eyebrows, questioning. Maya reiterated, quoting her mother's notebooks: "The films that you, the 'anonymous agent of the unattributable act' made, that caused the heads to be toppled, to decompose, to become the 700-meter-high flowers—did anyone ever know that it was you? Did you ever talk with anyone about it, how it happened? That you were *the catalyst*?"

Jane's face was a surprised question mark. She shook her head.

"But what about the crocosmia," Maya asked. "What about the flowers? Why did they grow in the capitals where the heads of state had died? Why did they grow to be so large, how was it they had appeared in the world exactly as they had appeared in your animations?"

"We made work to instantiate and bring about what states failed to," Jane whispered, haltingly, her voice failing. Maya lay down in the bed next to her and got as close as she could to listen. She had felt so old for so long, but now, a daughter again, she felt practically vigorous.

"The Union of Socialist Republics formed after the revolution in Russia in 1917 and what was their first mistake? Forming a state made of small nations, enclosures within enclosures, distorting socialism into a grid. The question was how to travel a road away from extinction, built upon extinction? How to undo the road; to find the beach underneath?" She paused to rest. Words came on a wave of emotion and her weary voice grew clear. "There were many millions who dedicated their lives to the Great Turning. We called it *cultivating the gardens of transformation*.

"In those years, I worked alone. I was responsible for

composting and signifying the many-in-one and the one-in many. Others worked in groups. There was the Iris Collective who cultivated the visionary valence, focused on producing poetic and pragmatic images of change for the better. The Gladiolas, in the celebrant mood, brought sublime fashion and festivity to protests and strikes. And of course, the Rosas, who helped me to raise you." She paused here, stirred. "Their educational projects fostered complexity—becomings."

Maya felt as if she was inside of something spinning, a washing machine. A careening car, a boat turned upside down had entered her mind. She felt tingling all throughout her body, a sudden cold in her belly, tightness in her sternum and throat: the old air hunger.

She saw how she *had not seen*, had missed the other flowerings. She had tunnel-visioned, only seeing her mother's contribution, when it was just one among many.

Maya passed out that afternoon and slept for three hours. When she opened her eyes, she was young again, looking at the ceiling while a hot claw carved again and again at her heart, in an agony of longing for Jane. When she remembered her mother was in the next room, she marveled at that feeling in her body. She had forgotten what it was like, and now her body reminded her, time-traveled back to her younger self, *still* trying to make sense of her mother's disappearance.

It came to her in this trance of the early body that she had hidden the truth from herself *because only the salvation of the whole world could justify her abandonment*. Messianism was the sense Maya had made of it; only if Jane had sacrificed Maya for the sake of everyone and everything could her vanishing be rationalized.

And Maya of the present realized that Maya of the past had decided, then and there, to believe this: that her mother had saved the world. She realized (she felt her whole body taken over with a wave of noiseless laughter) that her decision to live so much in solitude and to be so silent in company was a way to avoid being around others who would have challenged her version of reality. It was a decision to never know that one person could not save all beings, that transformation pivoted precisely on the opposite of the metaphysics of The One, which was the point of the symbolic beheadings of the so-called "world leaders," and that it took innumerous acts of care over decades and centuries, working together to get through the slim bottleneck, coming out the other side and escaping extinction to regenerate a habitable planet, their own damaged and wounded earth, to bring back species and support those that had newly emerged, evolutions of form, and that Jane was but one who had worked towards this, in concert with others.

Maya wrote about the power of her mistaken thought.

Thoughts are events, and they cause events as ceaseless and countless as a teeming anthill—thoughts projected; thought projects. Some people come together and turn their shared thoughts into social ideals. They project their thoughts into the world with so much force that the world is forever altered. Others, like me, hold onto a single thought and see everything through that prism.

§

Jane's energy diminished by the hour. She slept most of the time. She became more and more subtle, more and more sensitive to every alteration, every drop of water, crumb of food, every slender ray of light, breeze. She quivered like a leaf, gave looks as tiny and pointed as the smallest sewing needle, offered brief, light touches that sent waves of calm, rosy warmth through Maya's body. Each second was more tentative and precarious than the last.

In dying Jane reminded Maya of a vulnerable seedling, easily destroyed. Caring for her was a matter of setting aside initiative. The seedling of death needed to be allowed to grow backwards into the earth in its own time, without being rushed, trampled, or exhorted.

Jane asked Maya to read to her. Maya read poems, koans, stories. One day Jane spontaneously recited lines of poetry—

The room is dying honey and linden
Where drawers opened in mourning
The house blends with death
In a mirror whose lustre is dimming.

In case 17 from *The Book of Equanimity* Maya read: "If there is even a hair's breadth of difference, heaven and earth are clearly separated." "That's it," Jane said. "Like when I took your hand as a child, to cross the street. And when we got to the other side of the road, you dropped it and skipped on by yourself. Life is a child who goes on without you."

Life is a child, Maya thought, *but you are the one who went on without me.*

Life is what leaves you.

Every day Maya woke to rain. Water poured down and there

was no staving it off. She would get out of bed, check on Jane, put on a coat and rubber boots and circle the house, loving, as always, despite herself, the sound, feeling, and smell of inordinate rain. Wide rivulets in slippery clay made numberless tiny waterfalls, sweeping soil downhill, particle by particle.

The day before Jane died, she lay in bed with Maya sitting next to her in a chair. Maya told Jane that she was afraid. Jane said, “What if I told you we would be together again, after you also let go of your body?”

“Then I would be excited for my own death.”

“We will make up for lost time in the next world.”

They held hands all afternoon. Maya fell asleep in her chair.

Maya woke to a crash and felt the earth shake. The rain had stopped, and the sun was out. She went to investigate and found an enormous moss-covered limb from the largest of the big leaf maples had crashed down, opening a new part of the ravine below the house to the sky.

She examined a frilled turkey tail fluttering out from the stump of a tree, like an ear or a skirt. The morning light haloed the farther woods as the sun rose. Branches moved in every possible direction, up, out, sideways, downward, crisscrossing, fallen, just beginning, looking, seeking, moving everywhere to find space for proliferating tiny needles, flat and hand-like if cedar, chaotic like a broken thumb piano if hemlock.

A cedar branch leaned over her like a concerned friend. The dogwood in flower was cognizant, as was the Douglas fir, hemlock, cedar, Pacific yew, big leaf maple, alder, huckleberry, vine maple, and so many kinds of lichen, fungi, and moss she wouldn't know where to begin. They worked to respond to changes moment after moment that used to happen over entire seasons.

The light spread and moved across the forest, then withdrew as clouds passed. Alternation is the meaning of pattern. It's cold when the sun withdraws, leaves are laced with shadow where the sun is indirect, lighter, and warmer where it bejewels. Where the rays don't penetrate, an evenness, the broad, ordinary, unspecified light of a regular day. Then, the specificity of piercing, gleaming panes of cleaving light, glamorous patches of gold and white in the understory of shadow.

We are in their company, the ancients, we are their people, being mortal.

We're in their company, that of the stars and of the ancestors, and that of dogs, bats, and butterflies who never did dwell in an "animal kingdom," who, folded into a flowering underworld, wear green capes of moss and lichen, have minds of soil crowned with bones and memories, rocks and fossils, species' debris.

One pocket of soil home to millions of organisms. Where we do not see them there are the animalcules, repairing invisibly in opaque boiling vents of the world-garden. All forms are linked. A knee is like a muscled bend in a hillside. A tightness in the bone grown brittle is like a branch on its way to being a stick, everything aging together, all the time. The ravine's erosion mirrored the decay of her own memories.

All moments are linked. Does the next moment take something away from the one before?

For a long time, we are alive. The longest time of all is childhood when time is still unreal. Then death is nothing, or miniscule, a hole between gleaming dots in another star system.

7.

The sun had set, and the musicians were packing up. The cooperators of the café had decided to close for the evening. A few people were heading west to plant willows near a vast marsh where, they told Maya, only one grass had been grown for two generations of industrial dairy farming. Now birds, spiders, butterflies, turtles, beaver, spatterdock, and willow were returning.

She descended with the others back to ground. She made her way slowly to the learning center at the foot of the flower. She was curious to see how the locality represented the correlation between the deaths of the seven heads of state and the emergence of the seven flowers.

There was a crowd in the learning center and Maya had that feeling she always had in crowds, a sensation of disappearing, as if in a dream, becoming nameless and unknown. In earlier years that blur into sameness with others had, paradoxically, made her feel uncomfortably uncertain about what personhood was. It was always so hard to know herself, to know where she stood. There was nothing to hold onto. In solitude she didn't notice it.

But now, at her age, she enjoyed the drift of crowds. She had nothing to be afraid of anymore, least of all being nothing. She took pleasure in this collective patterning, becoming a flock, following along, though people tended to make way for such an elderly person as her, slowing their pace and mirroring her.

As expected, the wall texts that accompanied archival videos of the unprecedented growth of the flowers, and the news stories of what had befallen the seven heads, could not link the simultaneous events causally in any direct way. It was instructive to see the similarities in how each of the state apparatuses tried to explain what had happened to their authoritarians and even to resurrect them. At first, they scrambled to maintain social control. What a violent thing a prototype can be, Maya thought.

Maya wandered, reading and looking. There were hundreds of documents all saying the same thing, over and over.

Certain phrases stood out to her: "We don't know *how*. But there is clearly, in all of this, a *why*." "The etymology of capital, *capita*, head, as in heads of cattle, reveals how slaughter and profit were imbricated in the mind of capitalism." "A pragmatic utopian's work is never done." "The contradiction . . . is the criterion of the real."

Videos showed how the seven headless be-suited bodies tottered and froze. Brainless, mouthless, they had no last breath to draw.

Maya walked into a gallery filled with children's art, preserved from the time. One youth had written a fable that was most exact.

The people climbed to the high mountains and saw the world burning and flooding and everyone going hungry. They were angry and sad. They asked the mountains what to do and the mountains said, have faith, and gave them clay. They made dolls out of those who wanted to own it all. They cut off the heads of the dolls and the heads became seeds. They buried the heads in the ground which grew into red flowers. Once the the heads were gone, the people knew just what to do.

NOTES

"Of all the words / they've used for water / starlight was the first" is from an unpublished poetry collection *Abyss* (2024) by Dylan Desmond, by permission from the author.

"Every second was a narrow gate through which the messiah could enter" is paraphrased from "On the Concept of History" (1942) by Walter Benjamin.

The question "What services, what agencies were missing?" in relation to interdisciplinary architecture as health care is inspired by Robert Kocik, "The Prosody Building (A Plan for Expanding the Role of Poets)," in *Supple Science* (ON Contemporary Practice, 2013), 137–55.

See more about Mohsen Lihidheb's grief-work, "Memory of the Sea" here: T. Haney, L. Fadel, S.B. Brahim, & C. Harbage, "A Tunisian artist is hoping to keep the memories of migrants alive," *NPR*, December 21, 2022.

The "distant turning toward the distant" is from Mahmoud Darwish, *In the Presence of Absence* (Archipelago Books, 2011).

The Mike Davis interview referenced was in the *Los Angeles Times* on July 25, 2022. Davis died three months later to the day, October 25, 2022.

"Forms are everywhere structuring and patterning experience" is from *Forms: Whole, Rhythm, Hierarchy, Network* by Caroline Levine (Princeton University Press, 2015).

The passage "And I only am . . . forever prevails over the 'I am'" is from "Rams: Uninterrupted Dialogue—Between Two Infinities, the Poem" (2004), Derrida's close reading of a Paul Celan poem, "Vast, Glowing Vault" (1967).

The essays by Walter Benjamin and Theodor Adorno referenced here are, respectively, "On the Concept of History" (1942) and "Theses Against Occultism" (1947).

The idea of the "social command" is from *How Are Verses Made?* by Vladimir Mayakovsky (Cape Editions, 1970).

The notion of the "historical present as impasse" and the "lack of genres for transition" is from Lauren Berlant's *Cruel Optimism* (Duke, 2011).

The phrase "We clamor for the right to opacity for everyone" is from "For Opacity" in *Poetics of Relation* (University of Michigan Press, 1997) by Martinican philosopher and poet Édouard Glissant and translated by Betsy Wing.

The riff on mistaking effects for causes is indebted to Karen E. Fields and Barbara J. Fields' book *Racecraft: The Soul of Inequality in American Life* (Verso, 2012) in which they argue that "race" is an ideology, rather than a biological fact, and therefore that "race" is an *effect* of racism, not a cause. Because "race" is commonly reified as the cause of racism, they argue, there is a misunderstanding about what racism stems from, which, they assert, is not something called "race" but rather, exploitation and domination. "Race" doesn't therefore precede racism, but comes *after* the racism which it, in turn, is rooted in, and inseparable from. In this sense, in the Fields' account, the *concept* of "race" is itself a symptom of racism.

The idea that beauty is "purposeless purposiveness" is from Kant's *Critique of Judgement* (1790).

The citation from Martin Uman is in an article in *Qui Parle* called "Nature's Queer Performativity" by Karen Barad. Vol. 19, no. 2 (Spring/Summer 2011), 121–58.

The phrase "to think the less interesting thought" comes from J.M. Coetzee's *Elizabeth Costello* (Secker & Warburg, 2003) and before that, *The Lives of Animals* (Princeton University Press, 1999), in which he critiques experiments in "animal intelligence" which reduce test subjects to the level of the experiment, forcing them by their reductive and unreflexive structure to "think the less interesting thought."

The concept of the tyrant as "white clown" comes from *On Clowns: The Dictator and the Artist* (Grove Press, 1992) by Norman Manea.

The following passage in section two is from "No Small Matter: Mushroom Clouds, Ecologies of Nothingness, and Strange Topologies of Spacetimemattering" by Karen Barad, in *Arts of Living on a Damaged Planet* (University of Minnesota Press, 2017), edited by Anna Tsing, Heather Swanson, Elaine Gan, and Nils Bubandt:

Injustices need not await some future remedy, because 'now' is always already thick with possibilities disruptive of mere presence. Each moment is thickly threaded through all other moments, each a holographic condensation of specific diffraction patterns created by a plethora of virtual wanderings, alternative histories of what is/might yet be/have been. Re-membering, then, is not merely subjective, a fleeting flash of a past event in the inner workings of an individual human brain; rather, it is constitutive part of the field of spacetimemattering.

"Every truth has the structure of a fiction" is from Jacques Lacan's seminar, *The Ethics of Psychoanalysis (1959–1960)*, Book VII.

The concept of a "democracy of incommensurables" is from Jean-Luc Nancy. He poses it in *After Fukushima: The Equivalence of Catastrophes* (Fordham University Press, 2014).

In book 9 of Homer's *The Odyssey* Odysseus tells the Cyclops Polyphemus, who has abducted him to his cave and is planning to eat him, that his name is Nobody. He then attacks the Cyclops who cries out. Overheard by other Cyclopes and asked if he needs help, Polyphemus replies that "nobody" is attacking him and so the others don't come to his aid, allowing Odysseus to prevail and escape.

"A real subjection is born mechanically from a fictitious relation" is from "Panopticism" in *Discipline and Punish: The Birth of the Prison* (Pantheon Books, 1977) by Michel Foucault, 1926–1984.

The entire passage beginning "Luther removed the servitude of devotion . . ." and ending with ". . . their priestly nature" is from Marx, *Critique of Hegel's "Philosophy of Right"* (Cambridge University Press, 1970), 131. First published Paris, 1844.

"The Defeat of the Lords of Xibalba" is excerpted from a translation from the K'iche' of the *Popol Vuh* by Michael Bazzett (Milkweed, 2018), 194–5.

The references to liveable hemispheres are from *Nomad Century: How Climate Migration Will Reshape Our World* (Flatiron Books, 2022) by Gaia Vince.

The passage "When St. Boniface cut down the tree that was venerated as sacred by the Saxons, the bystanders expected some fearful event to follow upon the sacrilege. But nothing happened, and the Saxons accepted Baptism" is from *The Future of an Illusion* (Hogarth Press, 1962) by Sigmund Freud, 1856–1939.

The quotations in the passage ". . . often as not manifesting in a renewed 'over-estimation of psychic processes' which Freud described as the cause of the invention of religion, an over-estimation in which the neurotic, an 'animistic soul' is prey to the belief that she 'can change the outer world by a mere thought' and where the spirit's 'flightiness and mobility, its faculty of leaving the body, of permanently or temporarily taking possession of another body . . . characteristics which remind us unmistakably of the nature of consciousness' . . ." are from chapter three of Sigmund Freud's *Totem and Taboo* (Moffat, Yard, Co., 1918.), translated by A. A Brill from the Sigmund Freud Collection (Library of Congress).

The sentence "This unity was older than language, older than biota, older than matter—itself derived from consciousness, according to Max Planck" is drawing on an interview in which Planck is quoted as saying "I regard consciousness as fundamental. I regard matter as derivative from consciousness. We cannot get behind consciousness. Everything that we talk about, everything that we regard as existing, postulates consciousness." ("The Observer", 1931)

The phrase "ecological democracy" is from Vandana Shiva, *Earth Democracy: Justice, Sustainability, and Peace* (South End Press, 2005).

The phrase *obstructed the passage of time she was no longer in* is paraphrased from Rosmarie Waldrop's *Otherwise Smooth* (above/ground press, 2013). The full sentence is: "Now you obstruct the passage of time you're no longer in, and the clocks risk stopping."

"The inner reason of their life is money; and it is a kind of reason with very strong teeth and a hearty digestion" is from Robert Musil, *The Man Without Qualities* (Perigree Books, 1980).

"Gender is the extent we go in order to be loved" is from a personal note from Robert Glück.

The phrase "autonomous zones" refers here to self-governed, self-declared autonomous groups and regions, such as the Zapatistas in Chiapas, ZADs ("zone to defend") in France, and Rojava.

Universe as dodecahedron is from "Dodecahedral space topology as an explanation for weak wide-angle temperature correlations in the cosmic microwave background" by Jean-Pierre Luminet et al., published in *Nature* 425, (October 2003): 593–5.

"The room is dying honey and linden / Where drawers opened in mourning / The house blends with death / In a mirror whose lustre is dimming" is from *Les etoiles dans la main* (Seghers, 1954) by Jean Bourdeillette.

The koan cited is from the *Shoyoroku*, translated as *The Book of Equanimity*, a book of koans by Hongzhi Zhengjue (1091–1157) compiled by Wangsong Xingxiu (1156–1246) first published in 1224:

Case 17:

Attention! Hogen asked Administrator Monk Shuzan, "If there's even a hair's breadth of difference, heaven and earth are clearly separated. How do you understand this?" Shuzan replied, "If there's even a hair's breadth of difference, heaven and earth are clearly separated." Hogen said, "If that's so, how could you understand it?" Shuzan answered, "I am just this. How about you Osho?" Hogen remarked, "If there is even a hair's breadth difference, heaven and earth are clearly separated." At that, Shuzan bowed low.

"Contradiction is . . . the criterion of the real" is from *Gravity and Grace* (Librairie PLON, 1947) by Simone Weil.

ACKNOWLEDGMENTS

Thanks first and foremost to Nightboat Books including my kind, intelligent, and patient editor Lindsey Boldt as well as Stephen Motika, Jaye Elizabeth Elijah, Emily Bark Brown, Kit Schluter, Lina Bergamini, Dante Silva, and Morgan Levine who made this book possible. Deep gratitude for the generosity and insights of readers Evelyn Hampton, Annika Rausch, Eugene Lim, Thalia Field, Eirik Steinhoff, and Amanda Davidson. I am grateful for illuminating conversations about *Crocosmia* in various stages with Kelly Krumrie, Siloh Radovsky, Anne de Marcken, Jeff Champlin, Brian Teare, and Andrea Lawlor. Cassie Thornton's Feminist Economics Department and Hologram, and Jeanne Dodds's art and activism on behalf of endangered species and eco-systems, are part of the fabric of this book. Thank you to my friends and family, living and dead, especially my parents for their dedication to the liberation movements to which they committed their lives. I honor Joanna Macy, from whom the concept of the Great Turning originates, as well as the tutelary spirits of Simone Weil and Walter Benjamin who both died abjectly, war-torn, trying to cross over (as it were) or even *cross out* abysses of human confusion, impasses of the most painful injustices. We continue to learn from your fervent, messianic love: *Contradiction experienced to the very depths of the being tears us heart and soul.*

MIRANDA MELLIS is the author of the novel *Crocosmia*; three novellas, *The Revisionist*, *The Spokes*, and *The Quarry*; and a short-story collection, *None of This Is Real*. Her poetry and nonfiction books and chapbooks include *The Revolutionary*, *Demystifications*, *Unconsciousness Raising*, and *Materialisms*. She is the co-author of two book-length dialogues: *The Instead* with Emily Abendroth and *Passing Through* with Rick Moody. With Tisa Bryant and Kate Schatz, she was a founding co-editor at The Encyclopedia Project. She grew up in San Francisco and now lives in the woods of the Pacific Northwest where she is a professor at The Evergreen State College.

NIGHTBOAT BOOKS

Nightboat Books, a nonprofit organization, seeks to develop audiences for writers whose work resists convention and transcends boundaries. We publish books rich with poignancy, intelligence, and risk. Please visit nightboat.org to learn about our titles and how you can support our future publications.

The following individuals have supported the publication of this book. We thank them for their generosity and commitment to the mission of Nightboat Books:

Kazim Ali, Anonymous (4), Ava Aviva Avnisan, Jean C. Ballantyne, Will Blythe, V. Shannon Clyne, Theodore Cornwell, Ulla Dydo Charitable Fund, Gisela Gamper, Photios Giovanis, Amanda Greenberger, David Groff, Parag Rajendra Khandhar, Katy Lederer, Shari Leinwand, Elizabeth Madans, Ricardo Maldonado, Ethan Mitchell, Caren Motika, Elizabeth Motika, Asker Saeed, The Leslie Scalapino - O Books Fund, Amy Scholder, Thomas Shardlow, Benjamin Taylor, Jerrie Whitfield & Richard Motika, Clay Williams

This book is made possible, in part, by grants from the New York City Department of Cultural Affairs in partnership with the City Council and the New York State Council on the Arts Literature Program.

NYC Cultural Affairs

NEW YORK STATE OF OPPORTUNITY. | Council on the Arts